CW00447864

Tales of the *Completely* Unexpected

Seven short stories of murder,
mystery, revenge, obsession, humour,
and the supernatural,
each with a twist to the ending

Written by Keith Plummer

Grosvenor House
Publishing Limited

This book is published by
Grosvenor House Publishing Ltd
Link House
140 The Broadway, Tolworth, Surrey, KT6 7HT.
www.grosvenorhousepublishing.co.uk

A CIP record for this book
is available from the British Library

ISBN 978-1-83975-784-6

This book is for my wife Ved and daughter Leena who, like guardian angels, have stood by me for longer than I can remember, always loving, always caring, always there.

Tales of the *Completely* Unexpected

This collection of short stories continues where Roald Dahl's *Tales of the Unexpected* finished and consists of the following tales of murder, mystery, revenge, imagination and the supernatural: -

In addition there is a bonus story at the end of this volume, a two-act tragedy entitled "Home Sweet Home"

Preface

The short stories featured in this book were inspired by Roald Dahl's Tales of the Unexpected.

Anglia Television's Tales of the Unexpected was first launched in 1979 and, with a galaxy of star names from both sides of the Atlantic, the series was an instant success and regularly topped the Saturday night viewing figures in the United Kingdom.

In all, there were 112 episodes, including 25 stories written by Roald Dahl himself; these were taken from two of his collections, Kiss, Kiss and Someone Like You.

I remember avidly watching this series and appreciating Dahl's mixture of suspense, horror and dark comedy and trying not to miss a single episode as home video was in its infancy and repeats of television programmes at that time were very rare.

It is with these fond memories and recollections, after more than forty years since original transmission and fortuitously stumbling across a DVD collection of all 112 stories, that I have been prompted to write this collection of short stories. They are presented in a similar vein to the original series but I have also introduced elements of revenge, obsession and the supernatural.

Writing these short stories has given me great satisfaction and I trust that you, my readers, will find great pleasure in reading these *Tales of the Completely Unexpected* and be prepared to be surprised, thrilled and even shocked!

The Cruise Bear

The Cruise Bear

"Looks like we'll soon be there," said Roger looking out of the window as the aircraft came into land and the ground seemed to rush up to meet the plane at an alarming speed, "we're about to touch the runway. There!" he said with obvious relief, as the wheels screeched and the aircraft's engines were thrown into reverse, and all the passengers were pressed back into their seats.

"Thank goodness for that," replied Gwendolyn, "I know we have to fly but I'm always glad when we're back on solid ground."

"Once we've cleared immigration and customs it's only about thirty minutes to the ship. We should be there in time for a quick look round before dinner. I can't believe we're going to be on the Arcadian Princess' maiden voyage. Just think, nobody before us will have been in our cabin."

* * *

"Well, it's certainly a magnificent ship, very sumptuous and luxurious. And, of course, it only takes 650 passengers so it should feel very different to our last few

3

cruises when there were more than 2,000 people on board."

"It certainly will," agreed Gwendolyn, "we should be able to make some good friends on this voyage. In the 10 years since we retired we've been on lots of cruises all over the world but none of the people we've met have ever stayed close friends. True, we've exchanged Christmas cards and the odd letter, but we've never met anyone who we've really wanted to remain close to."

"Time to check out the dining room," exclaimed Roger, "don't know about you but I'm feeling famished so it's a good thing we booked first sitting. It must be all that travelling that makes us feel so peckish."

"You're right. I'm feeling very hungry myself. One good thing about a ship of this size is that everything is near to hand. I wonder," reflected Gwendolyn as she descended the stairs towards the dining room, "what sort of people will be on our table?"

* * *

Roger and Gwendolyn entered the dining room and were shown to their table by one of the head waiters. They were immediately overwhelmed by the stunning décor and lavish furnishings in the room. From their table they looked out over the stern and had a good view of the port from which they had recently embarked. It was now rapidly receding into the distance.

"Looks like we're going to be treated to a magnificent sunset," said Roger and, as he took his place, he glanced at the other guests seated at the table. It was a table for eight persons and two other couples were already seated so he introduced himself and Gwendolyn.

"I'm Roger and this is my wife Gwendolyn."

"Pleased to meet you; my name's David and this is my wife Marie."

"And I'm Chris and this is my better half, Dot."

After these somewhat awkward introductions the three couples exchanged information about themselves. Unlike Roger and Gwendolyn the other guests were not retired. David and Marie were in their early fifties and in the pharmaceuticals industry and, by all accounts, seemed to be hypochondriacs, while Chris and Dot appeared to be a few years younger and owned their own mortgage broking business. Roger wondered whether they were alcoholics as they were already on their second bottle of wine and the waiter hadn't yet brought round the menus. What all of them round the table had in common, however, was that they shared a love of cruising and between them had been all over the world.

Suddenly Chris changed the subject of the conversation. "We're still two people short on this table. I hope they haven't missed the boat," but his attempt at a joke fell on deaf ears.

"Could be jet lag or something," piped up David but, as he spoke, a waiter showed a middle-aged woman to the table and they all fell silent as she took her seat.

"I don't believe what I'm seeing," thought Roger, "that woman's carrying a teddy bear. And just look at it! It's wearing a long-sleeved shirt, long trousers and socks and shoes. If I didn't know better I'd say she's dressed it up to conform to this evening's dress code which is smart casual. Must be my imagination, no one's that obsessed with a toy bear – are they?"

The teddy bear had also intrigued the other guests seated round the table but none of them said a word as the woman proceeded to extract a small metal frame from her handbag and place it on the vacant seat next to her. She then extended this metal frame and sat the bear on top of it so its head and shoulders were just above table-top height. Everybody at the table was fascinated by this behaviour and watched without uttering a single word.

This uncomfortable silence was broken by Roger, who introduced himself and Gwendolyn. The other two couples quickly followed with their introductions.

"I'm Marilyn," responded the woman, "Marilyn Bear, and this is Teddy," she added patting the bear on the head, "His name is really Edward but I call him Teddy and you can too if you like."

"Marilyn Bear!" thought Roger to himself, "and Teddy Bear! This woman's got to be taking the Mickey," but as he was about to challenge those names the waiter appeared at the table and handed out the evening's menus.

"Don't forget Teddy!" snapped Marilyn and a rather puzzled looking waiter, no doubt wanting a quiet life, placed a menu on the table in front of the bear and went off to speak to the Maitre d'.

"How absurd," thought Roger, "that woman must be a bit soft in the head but why on earth did the waiter go along with it?"

After a few minutes the waiter returned and took everyone's orders for starters and the main course. Marilyn ordered a soup for herself and, as the waiter collected the menu from in front of the bear, said that Teddy would have the salad. For the main course she also ordered roast lamb for herself and salmon for Teddy, adding that he was only allowed to eat red meat once a week.

Roger didn't know how to contain himself and tried his hardest not to look at Gwendolyn as he was afraid he would burst out laughing. Somehow he managed to remain calm and joined in with those round the table as they resumed their conversations but he couldn't resist trying to discover more about Marilyn.

"So, Marilyn, what do you do for a living?"

"Oh, I don't do anything," was the reply, "well, what I should have said is that I don't have to do anything. My parents died in a car accident a few years ago. They were both investment bankers and left me very well off indeed. I don't have any brothers or sisters so spend most of my time travelling. Sometimes I go on adventure holidays but, over the past couple of years, I've caught the cruise bug and so here I am. I used to travel a lot with my parents but, after they died, my companion has been Teddy. He goes everywhere with me, don't you Teddy?" and Marilyn picked him up, kissed him on the cheek, and put him back at the table.

This behaviour confirmed what Roger was thinking, "She *is* soft in the head! I knew it as soon as I saw her walk in with that silly bear." It also had an unsettling effect on the others seated at the table who didn't know where to look or what to say.

Luckily the waiter and his assistant returned at this point and began to serve the starters and there was great astonishment when a plate of salad was actually placed in front of the bear. While the starters were being consumed there was some small talk but all eyes were firmly fixed on the salad and the bear.

Everybody, with the exception of the bear, quickly finished their starter and the plates were duly collected by the waiter who, without a word, picked up the untouched salad from in front of the bear and took it away.

All eyes were again on the waiter and his assistant when the main courses arrived. As before the waiter served everybody in turn around the table and placed a plate containing some beautiful salmon fillets and steamed vegetables in front of the bear without making any comment whatsoever. During the meal conversation was muted but all eyes were once again on Marilyn and the bear. Marilyn ate all her food and left a plate so clean that it looked like it didn't need to be washed up, but the plate of food in front of the bear, which was a culinary delight, remained uneaten.

Soon the plates were cleared away, including the uneaten food in front of the bear, and the dessert menus were handed out by the waiters. "I'll have the soufflé," said Marilyn, "it's one of my favourites but Teddy will have the sugar free option; he's got to watch his figure!"

Several of those sitting round the table could hardly keep a straight face but Roger was worried about the waste of food, "I'm not going to say anything today," he thought, "after all it is the first night of the cruise, but if this waste continues then I'm going to have a word with that woman. It's not right that so much food should just go to waste."

Following the dessert course, teas and coffees were served, and Roger was rather relieved when Marilyn didn't order a drink for the bear. Soon, after the beverages had been drunk, those around the table began to make their way out of the dining room. Roger and Gwendolyn decided to go to the cabaret theatre straightaway, even though there was nearly an hour to go before the show, so they could get a good seat for the evening's performance. Once they had settled down Roger ordered some drinks; he was a firm believer in duty-free alcohol.

The theatre slowly filled up over the next half an hour or so but, about 15 minutes before the show was due to begin, what could be mistaken for a football crowd descended on the lounge and nearly every seat was suddenly taken. Roger made sure he and Gwendolyn had another drink to sustain them through the performance and, as he sat down, he saw that sitting in the front row opposite was none other than Marilyn and, on the seat next to her, was that bear. He had got into the habit of always referring to it as 'that bear' and refused outright to call it 'Teddy' or Edward.

Leaving the theatre after what had been a very good 'Welcome Aboard Show' by the ship's company of singers and dancers, Roger and Gwendolyn decided to take a stroll around one of the upper decks and marvel at the full moon before having an early night. It had been a long day and they wanted to be wide awake for what would be their first full-day at sea.

* * *

The next morning Gwendolyn woke first, opened the curtains and looked out onto the balcony, "What a glorious day! Bright sunshine and not a cloud in the sky," and she went out onto the balcony and stretched out on a sun-bed and gazed out to sea. "This is the life," she thought to herself, "should be able to put up with this for another couple of weeks."

"Beautiful, isn't it?" she exclaimed as Roger joined her, "Why don't we have breakfast and then go on the sun deck. We could do some sun-bathing, have a dip in the pool or even have a soak in the Jacuzzi."

"Sounds great to me," he agreed and they returned inside the cabin to get changed and go to breakfast.

* * *

"That swim was just what I needed to work off last night's meal and that breakfast. I don't know why but whenever I'm on a cruise I always eat far too much; just can't help myself."

"I'm the same," agreed Roger, "Look, the Jacuzzi's got no-one in it, let's relax for a bit," and he led the way up the short flight of steps that wound up to the Jacuzzi.

"I think an hour's much too long to be in here but I just don't want to get out. The water's so hot that even in this temperature with the sun high in the sky we're going to feel cold," worried Gwendolyn, but Roger remained unmoved until prodded rather harshly by Gwendolyn. However, just as they were about to get out of the Jacuzzi, they were joined by David and Marie.

"Hope you don't mind if we join you, but it looks so good in there. I can't believe you've got this Jacuzzi all to yourselves."

"No, not at all, please come in. Mind you the water's very hot. I suppose this lovely hot sunny weather has persuaded most people to sunbathe rather than indulge in the pools or hot tubs."

"Yes," replied Marie, "we've just been on the sundeck. We saw Chris and Dot up there but they were sitting at the bar rather than sunbathing. There are lots of people up there but still plenty of sun-loungers available if you want to go and get a tan."

"And." added David, "You'll never guess who we saw right at the front of that deck?" But, before Roger or Gwendolyn could answer, he volunteered, "Marilyn and that bear of hers!"

"Really," pondered Roger, "I suppose it goes everywhere with her, even when she's sunbathing. Matter of fact, I think we should get a bit of sun. We've got about an hour before lunch so let's try and get a bit of colour into our winter skin," and he and Gwendolyn rather reluctantly made their way out of the Jacuzzi and up towards the sun deck.

David and Marie had been correct. There were plenty of sun-beds unoccupied around the pool and on the sun deck and Roger and Gwendolyn soon found two next to each other. It was only when they sat up to put on some sun block that they looked towards the front of the ship and espied Marilyn. As David had said, lying on a sun-bed next to Marilyn was 'that bear'. It was fully stretched out and, much to Roger's astonishment, was wearing nothing but a pair of Speedo swimming trunks and a pair of Prada sunglasses. He looked at Marilyn who was obviously sound asleep and then he looked at the bear and finally sighed heavily before relaxing on his sun-lounger to soak up some sun.

* * *

After going to the afternoon's trivia quiz, and narrowly being beaten into second place by a team of obvious trivia fanatics, Roger and Gwendolyn decided to go and have another soak in the Jacuzzi. They thought it would relax them before dinner. They had been there for about half an hour and were both almost asleep with their eyes closed when a familiar voice called out, "Hello! How nice to see people we know. You won't mind if we join you will you?" and Roger looked up in horror to see Marilyn, holding her Teddy, climbing up the stairs and about to get into the Jacuzzi. However, before getting in, she placed Teddy on the outer edge of the tub as far away from the water as possible.

"Don't want you to get wet now, do we?" she said patting Teddy on the head and lowering herself slowly into the water.

"Why me?" wondered Roger, as he looked straight ahead of him at 'that bear', "Why am I being haunted by that silly bear?" It was then that his mischievous side took over and he said in a rather sarcastic tone of voice, "Isn't Teddy going to join us in here?"

"Certainly not!" retorted Marilyn, "He's not allowed to get wet. It might ruin him and that would never do. That's why I sit him right on the edge and tell him to be careful and not fall down those stairs," and Marilyn gave the bear a little wave.

After what seemed an age, but which had in fact been only about 15 minutes, Roger and Gwendolyn made their excuses and left the hot tub, "See you at dinner,"

Marilyn shouted after them as they made their way down the stairs.

* * *

Roger and Gwendolyn were last to arrive at the table for dinner and soon joined in the ongoing conversations. Marilyn was present accompanied by Teddy who was wearing an immaculately pressed white shirt, black trousers and shiny patent leather shoes. "Quite the dandy," observed Roger and he forced himself to remain silent.

Events followed a similar pattern to the night before and, for each course, Marilyn ordered food for Teddy which remained uneaten. Watching this Roger was becoming increasingly frustrated at what he considered to be a complete waste of good food and couldn't understand why no-one else round the table seemed to be in the least concerned. Finally, when a rack of lamb with some exquisite glazed vegetables were left completely untouched by 'that bear' and taken away by the waiter, Roger could contain himself no longer and erupted angrily towards Marilyn, "Don't you think it's a waste ordering good food for that bear and letting it all go uneaten. You should be ashamed of yourself!"

Marilyn was quick to respond, "You can talk! Look at your own plate. You haven't eaten everything so why complain about poor Teddy here."

"That's not the point. We've all paid good money to come on this cruise so if we choose to leave our food then in a sense it's our own money we're wasting. It's different with that bear; he hasn't paid anything but is wasting good food that could be eaten by someone else!"

"That's where you're wrong," answered Marilyn in a surprisingly conciliatory tone, "Teddy comes on this cruise as a fully fare-paying passenger. I paid the same for him as I paid for myself and, I dare say, as much as you paid for yourself and Gwendolyn. Matter of fact we're in one of the largest suites on this ship so I've most probably paid more for him to come on this cruise than you two together. So, just as you can choose to leave your food, so can my Teddy," and Marilyn patted the bear on the head as if reassuring him.

This revelation stunned all those round the table and there was an icy silence that was eventually broken by Roger, "You're asking us to believe that you paid several thousand Pounds for that bear to come on this cruise! Why not just pack him in your suitcase like anybody else would do?"

"Pack him in a suitcase! Certainly not," replied Marilyn who picked up Teddy and placed him carefully on her lap, "My Teddy will never be packed in a suitcase. He's too precious for that. Whenever we travel together he gets a seat on the plane next to me," and she kissed the bear lightly on its cheek.

"You're telling us that you paid for that bear to have a seat on the plane coming out from London; I don't believe it!"

"It's true. I always travel first class and Teddy does as well. You get much better service that way and besides Teddy enjoys it; he couldn't travel any other way."

Roger was stunned at this revelation. He had heard of musicians who played large instruments, such as the cello, paying for a seat so the instruments didn't have to travel in the aircraft's hold but a bear, a common toy bear occupying a first class seat; that was ridiculous. This did, however, get him thinking and his mind wandered back to the overnight flight. He was furious; there he was in economy class sitting almost upright trying to get some sleep while at the front of the aircraft that bear had a first class bed all to itself! He finished the remainder of the meal in silence and he and Gwendolyn left as soon as the meal was over.

That night in their cabin Roger could talk of nothing else but 'that bear' until Gwendolyn, tired of the whole subject, made him go to sleep.

* * *

The next day the ship docked and the majority of the passengers took the opportunity to go ashore. Some had booked shore excursions through the ship's tour office while others had made their own arrangements. Roger and Gwendolyn had been to this port before so decided to take a local bus into a nearby town that they rather liked. Chris and Dot also went ashore and immediately headed for the comfort of the nearest beach bar, while David and Marie went in search of a local pharmacy.

It was on the return journey that things took a turn for the worse. Roger and Gwendolyn had to run and just made the local bus as it departed from the small town. They were the last to board and, as they looked around the single deck vehicle, they noticed that all the seats had been taken and they were the only ones standing. It was then that Roger noticed Marilyn sitting towards the rear of the bus with Teddy placed on the seat next to her. He and Gwendolyn made their way to the rear but, instead of offering to give up Teddy's seat, Marilyn just exchanged a few words with them and went back to staring out of the window. Annoyed at this apparent lack of manners Roger asked if Marilyn could put Teddy on her lap so that Gwendolyn could have a seat for the return journey that he knew would take about half an hour.

"Certainly not," retorted Marilyn rather indignantly at the very thought of it and pointed to a ticket attached to the bear's paw, "I've paid good money for this seat and besides Teddy doesn't travel very well. He can't sit on my lap and has to have his own seat," and she rolled up the cuffs of the bear's shirt sleeves to reveal a travel band on each wrist.

Gwendolyn was amused at this and only just managed to stifle a giggle but Roger felt humiliated and angry. He was getting fed up with both Marilyn and 'that bear' and was beginning to plot how he could get rid of 'that bear' for good. Besides, he and Gwendolyn had spent a lot of time on their feet in the scorching sun exploring the town and he knew Gwendolyn was tired and could really do with a seat on this very hot and stuffy bus.

* * *

Things didn't get any better that evening. This was the first formal night of the cruise and both Roger and Gwendolyn enjoyed the dressing up. They believed it made them feel better and they liked to see what the other guests were wearing and often they got ideas for future cruises. Although both were in their mid-sixties they were fairly trim and looked good for their age. Roger put his dinner suit on and Gwendolyn put on a stunning white cocktail dress that made her look ten years younger.

"You look absolutely gorgeous my love," said Roger and he kissed his wife on the cheek as she prepared to leave the cabin.

"You don't scrub up too badly yourself," she joked, and they left the cabin hand in hand, "Do you want a photograph taken with the captain this time?"

"No, I don't think so. We've got so many and we never look at them so let's just go straight into dinner."

"Agreed," nodded Gwendolyn and they took the lift down to the dining room. On the way they looked at what the other passengers were wearing and Roger said, "I think we compare very favourably, both in terms of how we're dressed and not looking our ages."

When they arrived in the dining room the others were already seated at the table apart from Marilyn and the bear. "Perhaps she's not coming tonight," Roger thought to himself, and then engaged in conversation with David and Marie who, as was their habit, laid out a long line of pills that they consumed with every meal.

It was Chris who broke the news, "Here comes Marilyn with that bear and you won't believe this!"

Roger turned to look towards the dining room entrance and his heart sank. Marilyn, who must have been in her late forties, was wearing a most expensive designer dress that would not have been out of place on the body of a top model in any one of London's most trendy nightclubs. But 'that bear', he couldn't believe his eyes. 'That bear' was dressed in a tuxedo, complete with royal blue bow tie and cummerbund, a frilly dress shirt and expensive black leather shoes.

Once again, those on the table sat in silence as Marilyn carefully placed Teddy on his chair, and picked up the menu.

"That outfit looks more expensive than mine," Roger grumbled to himself as he studied the bear's clothes.

The meal passed without incident and nobody around the table commented on the food wasted by the bear but a further humiliation was in store for Roger.

After the meal he and Gwendolyn went for a drink with Chris and Dot and forgot that the show was starting 15 minutes earlier than usual so, when they arrived in the theatre, there were few seats remaining and nowhere could two next to each other be found. Then Roger noticed Marilyn and 'that bear' sitting two rows from the front with an unoccupied seat next to 'that bear'. They made their way to the row of seats and Roger asked if Marilyn would be prepared to hold

Teddy on her lap so he and Gwendolyn could sit together.

"Certainly not," stressed Marilyn echoing her words on the bus earlier in the day, "Teddy likes to have a good seat so he can see the show and I'm not having him miss any of it."

"Very well," sighed a very weary Roger, and he left Gwendolyn sitting next to 'that bear' and found a vacant seat a few rows behind. He sat back in the seat and eagerly awaited the show but his mind was filled with thoughts of 'that bear' and he just couldn't settle or get into the show. Finally, he made up his mind, "That blasted bear has to go! And I'm going to get rid of it. Tomorrow I'm going to throw it over the side and I know just how I'm going to do it." He smiled and settled back in his seat; at last he could enjoy the remainder of the show.

* * *

At breakfast the next day Roger outlined his plan of action to Gwendolyn. She was beginning to think that this obsession with the bear was getting out of hand but Roger could not be persuaded to change his mind.

"It's quite simple, really," he explained, "we've another day at sea today and I plan to spend the morning lazing around in the swimming pool. I can keep an eye on the hot tubs from there and, sooner or later, Marilyn is going to go for a soak in one of them. When she's the only one in the tub and is relaxing with her eyes closed then I'm going to creep up those stairs and grab 'that bear' and throw him over the side as far as I can. She always puts him right on the edge so he doesn't get wet so I can easily reach him without her noticing until it's too late and he's gone for good."

"If you say so, dear," nodded Gwendolyn, but deep down she was beginning to worry about Roger's sanity. She had never before seen him so obsessed and determined in all their years of marriage and added, "Be careful. I know it's a hot sunny day but the sea is somewhat choppy today."

It was later that morning as Roger was lazily swimming on his back in the pool that he noticed Marilyn and 'that bear' make their way up to one of the Jacuzzis. Sure enough, after a few minutes, the other people in there had gone and Marilyn was alone with Teddy whom she had placed right on the edge by the stairs. About 15 minutes later Marilyn had her eyes closed and Roger knew he had to seize his chance; it was now or never!

Roger left the pool and made his way to the stairs leading up to the Jacuzzi. He quietly made his way almost to the top and peered over into the hot tub. Much to his satisfaction 'that bear', complete with swimming trunks and designer sunglasses, was only a few inches from his outstretched hand. Time to make his move but, as he leaned forward, the ship suddenly lurched to one side and the bear fell straight into his hands. He all too willingly grabbed it but his wet feet slipped on the stair treads and with the swaying of the ship he was unable to prevent himself from falling. He let out a yell as he plummeted head-first towards the deck below and fell silent as blackness enveloped him.

* * *

Roger slowly opened his eyes. Where was he? Everywhere was so quiet. Then suddenly it all came back to him. The fall, yes the fall, was he injured? Was there any permanent damage? He tried to get up from the bed but try as he might Roger couldn't move; his body and limbs simply refused to obey the commands of his brain. He tried to speak but, once again, no sound was forthcoming. He began to panic and moved his eyes from side to side in the vain hope that if anyone was there they might see this small movement. He tried to focus and eventually fixed his gaze on a figure at the foot of the bed. Slowly Gwendolyn came into focus.

"Roger! Roger!" she repeated, "You've come round at long last," and she came and stood by his side. "You don't know how long I've waited for this moment. It's been six months and they all said you wouldn't make it. The doctors kept urging me to turn off your life support system but I refused. I knew with your iron constitution you'd pull through somehow." She moved closer and held his hand tightly in her own.

Roger again tried to move but to no avail. The only thing he could do to show Gwendolyn that he was able to hear her was to move his eyes fractionally and blink occasionally.

"I know it must be difficult for you to accept, particularly after the active life you've lived, but the doctors say that given time you should regain some movement in your limbs. They're hopeful that you should get some feeling back in your arms and hands but doubt that you'll ever walk again. I've been so worried about you. I can't tell you how wonderful it is to have you back again. I hope you can understand me," and after noticing a slight flicker in Roger's eyes she continued, "That's good, I'll update you on what's been happening and how we managed to fly you back home. Thank goodness we had good travel insurance or I don't know how I would have managed," and Gwendolyn went on to outline to Roger all that had happened to her during the last six months until she noticed his eyes had shut and he had slipped back into a deep sleep.

Later that day Roger awoke again and was reassured to see Gwendolyn sitting by his bedside reading a book. Gwendolyn at once grabbed hold of his hand, "Of course, it's at times like these that you find out who your real friends are. Most of our neighbours had given up on you and, as for your brother, he's only been to see you once. He says to let him know when there's any change in your condition. I don't think he cares about you at all.

Your accident has taught me the nature of true friendship and you'll never believe who's come to stay with us until you're better. We met them on the ship."

Roger cast his mind back to the cruise and the people at the dinner table, "It couldn't be Chris and Dot because they'd be too drunk to care for themselves let alone somebody else. No, it must be David and Marie. They're in the pharmaceutical business and no doubt will have views on my treatment. Yes, that's it, David and Marie."

Gwendolyn leant forward and said quietly, "It's Marilyn, she's been a rock over these last few months and I couldn't have coped without her. She's paid for you to have some of the best physiotherapists in the country. She's here now," and Gwendolyn moved to one side to reveal a smiling Marilyn.

"Roger, hello it's Marilyn. I can't thank you enough for saving my poor Teddy. If you hadn't caught him when the ship hit those rough seas and he fell off the Jacuzzi he would have been lost overboard. I don't know what I'd do without him! I'm going to make sure that I repay your kindness and do you know how I'm going to do it?"

Roger couldn't believe what Marilyn was saying. Not only had his plan apparently failed but he was being praised for saving 'that bear'. He stared in front of him at the two women, desperately trying to communicate, but to no avail.

"I'm going to make sure that you receive the best treatment available and look who's going to help me!"

Roger looked blankly on as Marilyn gave a big smile and, with a flourish worthy of any good magician, produced Teddy from behind her back. Teddy, wearing a doctor's long white coat and sporting a toy stethoscope around his neck!

The End

Wishing Well

Wishing Well - a well that has the supposed power of making a wish come true.

Wishing Well - giving encouragement and support.

Wishing Well

"Well, here we are," said Matt as they drove into the small village, "Long Hooton, and it looks just as lovely as in the estate agent's blurb."

"Yes," replied Natalie, "very quaint and picturesque. I do hope we can find our dream cottage here. I can't believe it's only two months to our wedding day and I don't want to end up living with my parents after we're married. I've almost given up hope of finding somewhere suitable. We've looked at so many cottages now and they're either too small or too expensive. I suppose that's the choice we have if we want to live in the countryside away from the town."

"I'm confident we'll soon find a home of our own; I have a good feeling about this place," said Matt as he parked the car on the side of the village green adjacent to the duck pond. "Let's go for a walk around. The estate agent said there were a couple of properties for sale in the village."

"You wouldn't think such a pretty village as this could be just a half-hour's drive from Colchester. It would be such a convenient location to live from a work point of view and we'd also be in easy reach of our parents."

"I like the way the church is situated at one end of the village and here, clustered round the village green, are a few cottages, the village shop, the Post Office and, of course, the village pub. 'The Plough and Wheatsheaf', not the most original of names but I suppose it sums up the rural nature here," added Matt, "Now, where's the first of those cottages?"

"Peace Cottage is near the pub over there," pointed Natalie gesturing towards the far end of the village green, "but it's semi-detached and I so wanted a detached cottage."

"A detached cottage would probably be outside our price range. I know we've been lucky with our parents giving us substantial sums towards our first house as a wedding present but we'll still need quite a large mortgage. I've done the calculations and we can't go over £300,000; that's the absolute limit. Normally that would get us a good four-bedroom detached property in Colchester but cottages in a pretty little village like this are bound to attract a premium."

Natalie looked around then exclaimed, "There it is. Over there to the side of the church, 'Wishing Well Cottage', and it looks absolutely charming."

The couple walked hand-in-hand across the village green over to the rear of the church. It was Sunday afternoon and the church was empty. They resisted the temptation to look inside and made their way straight to the cottage.

"Look at that! It's everything I ever wanted," mused Natalie, "from the lovely cottage garden, the climbing roses all over the front of the house, and the period windows and gables. And that solid oak front door; it's actually got a wishing well carved in the wood."

"I bet we can't afford it," Matt said rather cynically, "it looks expensive to me." The young couple stood at the small wooden front gate admiring the property but deep-down realising that it was probably too expensive for them.

"Let's head back to Colchester then. We might be able to get to the estate agents before they close. I think it's four o'clock on Sundays," said a rather dejected Natalie who had obviously fallen in love with the period cottage.

As they turned to make their way back across the village green a figure appeared over the boundary wall of the adjoining cottage and called out to them, "Going so soon! Would you like to have a look inside? I can see from the papers you're holding that you're house hunting. This really is a charming cottage and I'd like to have some neighbours again. The previous owners moved out nearly a year ago so it's high time the old place echoed to voices once again. I'm John Brooksbank, by the way, and I've got the keys if you've got a few minutes to spare."

"I'm Matt Clutterbuck and this is my fiancée Natalie Honeyball. Matt and Natalie."

"Yes, Natalie. I don't like it when we're referred to as Matt and Nat! Some of our friends just can't resist it."

"Quite so! Call me John," and without further ado John Brooksbank left his garden and joined them in front of the cottage. John was clearly in his late sixties but was dressed in trendy clothes and moved very sprightly for someone of his age. He fumbled in his trouser pockets and produced a bunch of keys from which he selected a rather large old fashioned key and placed it in the lock.

"Come inside and I'll give you the tour. I've lost count of just how many times I've done this over the last few months. Several people have put in offers on the cottage but none of them have been accepted. I think the previous owners are holding out for too much in the present market climate. Maybe you'll be lucky. I have a good feeling about you two," and John ushered them inside.

"Wow!" exclaimed Natalie as the door opened straight into the sitting room, "This is just what we've been looking for! Not only have we got exposed wooden beams, but there's brick flooring and a huge open fireplace. And it's got an inglenook into the bargain."

"There's a smaller room which is set out as a dining room and over here, through this door, is the kitchen. As you can see in contrast to the rest of the down stairs it's very up to date with all modern conveniences and appliances. It was installed just a few months before the property became vacant."

"It's fabulous," remarked Natalie, "I can't wait to see upstairs."

"Like most cottages there are only three bedrooms, two of them are furnished but the third one is completely empty, I think it used to be the nursery. The master bedroom has an en-suite and there is a family bathroom for guests or children. As is the case for the kitchen, the bathroom and en-suite were modernised just months before the previous owners left. As you can see no expense was spared on these two rooms. They spent a lot of money and time renovating and restoring the cottage as well as modernising the place and when they'd got it just how they wanted it they left to move back to London," sighed a rather melancholy John.

Matt and Natalie took the opportunity and wandered round the cottage on their own. They were lost for words; the cottage had been wonderfully restored and was full of the most charming and appropriate period furniture. It was with sadness that they thanked John for the tour of the property and made their way across the village green to their car.

Fastening her seat belt Natalie couldn't help herself, "I think I've fallen in love with that cottage. Let's get back to Colchester and speak to the estate agent. Let's hope it falls within our price range. I'll be so disappointed if we can't afford it."

On the journey back to Colchester the couple could speak about nothing else but 'Wishing Well Cottage' and their excitement mounted as they parked the car and hurriedly crossed the road to the estate agents, Hurrell & Hurrell.

"Mr Clutterbuck and Miss Honeyball, do come in and take a seat," exclaimed James Hurrell as the couple almost burst through the door, "Did you find anything suitable in Long Hooton? It's a lovely little village."

"We did," replied an excited Natalie, "but we think it might be just a bit too expensive for us."

"Wishing Well Cottage," added Matt, "we were absolutely blown away by it."

"A lovely property that's been on the market for nearly a year, if my memory serves me correctly, and I'm very surprised it hasn't been sold by now. Let me see," and James Hurrell quickly sifted through a pile of papers to the side of his desk, "Here we are. Oh!" and he paused, "Your budget is for properties in the range £250,000 to £300,000 so you're not going to like this. Wishing Well Cottage is currently on the market for £349,995."

"Yes, that's definitely too much for us. Even if we could raise that sort of money we'd have nothing left for furniture and fittings," acknowledged a despondent Natalie, "Looks like we'll have to keep looking."

"Don't worry," reassured James Hurrell, "Something's bound to come up. I'll see what else is on the market and send you the details in a day or so."

At that very moment the telephone started ringing so Matt and Natalie took the opportunity to leave the estate agents and made their way across the road to their car. They sat there in silence for a few minutes before Matt turned the key in the ignition. As he did so there was a loud tap on the rear window that startled them.

"Mr Clutterbuck!"

"It's the estate agent," said Matt looking over his shoulder, "What on earth can he want? Don't tell me he's found some other properties already!"

"Mr Clutterbuck, may I have a word with you and Miss Honeyball? Could you come back to the office please?" James Hurrell said rather insistently.

Reluctantly Matt and Natalie accompanied the estate agent across the road back to his office.

"What's this all about?" enquired Natalie once they were inside the office.

"Well, I don't quite know how to say this. It's never happened before."

"What hasn't?" questioned Matt.

"You may find this hard to believe but that telephone call as you were leaving the office was from the vendors. They've suddenly decided to drop the asking price for Wishing Well Cottage from £349,995 to £299,995."

"Are you serious?" exclaimed Matt, "Just like that, they've knocked £50,000 off the asking price?"

"That's correct. There was no explanation given but the asking price is now just within your price range. What do you say? Do you wish to proceed with the purchase of that property?"

Matt and Natalie had a hurried conversation in a corner of the office before announcing that they were more than happy to proceed with the purchase. It was a great weight off their minds and would allow them to concentrate fully on their wedding which was now only two months away.

James Hurrell took details of the couple's solicitors and undertook to start the conveyancing arrangements straight away. He was optimistic that occupation could take place immediately after the wedding as the cottage was empty and in this instance there was no chain of properties to buy and sell.

It was a very happy and contented Matt and Natalie who drove back to Colchester with news that they couldn't wait to break to their respective parents.

* * *

About a month later Matt and Natalie received a request from their solicitor to call in and see her about the purchase of Wishing Well Cottage as a matter of urgency. Intrigued, they left work early and rushed round to the offices of Bawtree & Bright.

"Come in and take a seat," exclaimed Miss Castleton as her secretary showed the young couple into her office. "You must be wondering why I wished to see you so urgently."

"I hope it's not bad news about the purchase," responded Natalie as she sat down awkwardly on the rather old-fashioned wooden chair, "we really don't want to lose that cottage."

"Quite the contrary, as a matter of fact, but I thought you should hear it from me in person rather than on the phone or a letter so there can be no doubt."

"No doubt about what?" enquired Matt.

"The furniture in the cottage," replied Miss Castleton.

"It's lovely. Most of it is antique and must have cost a fortune but it goes so well in that cottage. I don't think we'll be in a position to buy much furniture for a long time. I think we'll be making do with just a bed and a table and chairs," joked Natalie.

"Well, that's where you're wrong," emphasised the solicitor, and with a smile continued, "The vendors, Mr & Mrs Owen, wrote to me this morning and said that they have no use for the furniture and are prepared to sell it to you."

"Sell it to us," mused Matt, "but that furniture must be worth thousands of pounds. We're simply not in a position to stump up that sort of money."

"You don't have to. Mr & Mrs Owen say they understand that you are shortly to be married and wish you well and are prepared to let you have all the furniture and fittings in the cottage for the sum of £5.00."

"£5.00!" Exclaimed Matt and Natalie in unison, "£5.00!"

"That can't be right!" exclaimed Matt. "There must be a catch somewhere. I just can't believe that they would let all that wonderful furniture go for, well, nothing!"

"It's here in writing," confirmed Miss Castleton waving a letter in front of the by now very happy couple, "There's no catch. Shall I write and accept?"

"Yes please, and tell Mr & Mrs Owen that we accept their well wishes and are very happy to accept their very generous and most kind offer." Matt and Natalie could barely contain themselves and hugged each other tightly hardly believing their good fortune.

"I'll make sure it's all included in the contract of sale. Now there really is nothing more that needs to be done so far as the purchase is concerned. Hopefully we'll soon be in a position to exchange contracts and I'm confident that you'll be able to move into the cottage right after your wedding. Are you going on honeymoon?"

"Yes," replied Natalie, "we're spending a couple of weeks on a friend's boat on the Norfolk Broads. Things have been very hectic over the last few weeks what with the cottage and the wedding so it'll be great just to take time to relax and chill out with nothing to do. We can then move into the cottage and start work again refreshed. I can't believe it's all happening at once and everything's fitting into place so perfectly."

* * *

About six weeks later Matt and Natalie moved into Wishing Well Cottage. They had a good look round the inside then slowly wandered round the well stocked garden.

"I knew it!" exclaimed Natalie, "I knew there would be a wishing well somewhere in the garden."

"It's a well all right," agreed Matt, "but I don't know if it's a wishing well and why is it partially concealed by these bushes?"

Matt and Natalie fetched some tools from a small shed at the bottom of the garden, dug up the bushes, and threw them on top of a long-neglected compost heap.

"There what did I tell you? It looks just like a wishing well from all those fairy stories you read as a child. It's even got a bucket on a rope and there is actually water in the bottom so it is a proper well."

"Think I'll stick to water out of the tap, thank you."

"Spoil sport! Come on, let's go in. I can't wait to spent our first day and night in our own lovely little cottage," and Natalie led the way back inside.

Natalie cooked their first meal on the range in the kitchen and the young couple then spent the remainder of the evening in the sitting room cuddling each other on one of the period settees and watching television. They then showered and sorted out clean clothes for their first day back at work following their wedding and honeymoon. They went to bed feeling exhausted but excited that they had now spent their first day in the cottage of their dreams.

As soon as their heads touched the pillow they both fell asleep but Matt was forcibly awakened about an hour later by a very worried Natalie shaking him vigorously.

"Can you hear it?"

"Hear what?" mumbled a very drowsy Matt.

"Voices! There are voices coming from the sitting room. Listen!"

Matt sat bolt upright in the bed and listened, "You're right, there are voices in the sitting room. They're a bit muffled but it's as if two people are having a conversation and they're making no attempt to keep their voices down. Damn!" he exclaimed, "My mobile phone's downstairs. No choice, I'll have to go and find out what's it all about."

"But they might be burglars. They might have knives or weapons. Do be careful," implored Natalie.

"Well, I've got a surprise for them. There are a couple of old swords on the wall on the landing outside the bedroom; I'll take one of them," and without a further word Matt crept quietly onto the landing, took one of the swords, and gingerly went down the stairs. Natalie took the other sword and followed close behind.

"I can't make out what they're saying," whispered Matt, "but there are definitely at least two of them. The room's in darkness so we'll surprise them. On the count of three we'll rush into the room and switch on the light. Hopefully, that'll frighten them and we can see them off. Now," he whispered and slowly counted, "One, two, *three*!"

Matt and Natalie, still in their pyjamas, burst into the room and switched on the light but, much to their surprise, there was nobody there. They stood in the middle of the room and stared at each other in sheer disbelief.

"How stupid must we look," smiled Natalie, "standing here in our nightclothes brandishing swords in an empty room." But no sooner had she uttered these words then the voices started again and she immediately flung herself into Matt's arms.

"Hey, come on, it's only the radio," reassured Matt, and he extricated himself from Natalie's strong embrace and walked over to the far corner of the sitting room,

"There, that's solved that problem," and he switched the radio off.

"Well, that's a relief," sighed Natalie, "but I don't remember actually putting the radio on last night. If you recall we watched television all evening."

"Radios don't switch themselves on by themselves, do they? Come on, let's get back to bed. We don't want to be too tired for work tomorrow. After all, everyone will be expecting us to return refreshed. Besides, they'll want to know all about the wedding and the honeymoon."

The next night before going to bed Natalie made a point of making sure that the radio was switched off even though it hadn't been used that evening. She had had a very hard first day back in the office and was looking forward to a good night's sleep. Matt had also found it tiring going back to work so he too was after an early night.

Tiredness quickly overcame them and both Matt and Natalie were soon sound asleep but, just as the night before, Matt found himself being woken up after about an hour in bed by a very worried Natalie.

"Matt, Matt, wake up!" implored a very concerned Natalie, "I can hear voices again."

"Don't tell me it's that radio again," mumbled a seemingly unconcerned Matt, "You can go down and switch it off this time."

"It can't be the radio because I made sure it was off before we came up to bed."

"What else can it be?" replied Matt who, by now, was getting just a little bit fed up at being woken up two nights in a row, "But, if it'll make you happy, I'll go and have a look but this time I'm not taking the swords."

Once again muffled voices were clearly audible. Matt and Natalie crept down the stairs and burst into the sitting room. As before it was empty but, once again, the radio was switched on.

"That's impossible," stammered Natalie, "I made sure that radio was switched off before I came upstairs. How come it's on now?"

"It could be some sort of timer or it could just be a faulty switch."

"Well, it's giving me the creeps," said Natalie, and she promptly walked over to the radio, switched it off and pulled the plug out of its socket.

"Come on, let's get back to bed. Excitement's over for tonight!"

* * *

After their first two disruptive nights in the cottage things settled down and they managed to get some uninterrupted nights' sleep but Natalie was still a bit apprehensive every time they went to bed.

"Are you sure you'll be all right spending your first day in the cottage on your own?" said Natalie sarcastically, "I did promise the girls that I'd go shopping in Colchester with them."

"No problem," replied Matt, "I want to dig up that grass at the top of the garden and make a vegetable plot. My parents grow a lot of their own produce and I thought it would be a good idea for us to do the same."

"It will certainly keep you out of mischief until I return. Have fun," and Natalie kissed Matt on the cheek and made her way out to the car.

Digging up the patch of grass proved much harder than Matt had anticipated and took him into the early afternoon.

"Think I'll have a nice long soak in the bath. It will make a change from a shower and I can lay there and relax listening to some music."

Matt started to run the bath and while it was filling up he went into the sitting room and found his portable CD player. He selected a couple of his favourite CDs and plugged the machine into a socket on the wall outside the bathroom. He switched the player on and went back into the bathroom. However, just as he was about to get into the bath, the music stopped.

"Is that you Natalie? Are you home?" But there was no reply.

"Just like her to come back and switch my music off. Natalie!" He shouted, but once again there was no reply so Matt gingerly opened the door. There was nobody there, the cottage was in silence.

"That's odd," he thought, "it must have been her."

Matt put his dressing gown on and went downstairs and checked the doors; they were all locked. He came back up to the bathroom and once again switched the CD player on. He topped the bath up with hot water then, before getting in, went outside the room and checked that the CD player was still operating. He turned the volume up, returned to the bathroom and got into the bath.

"Lovely!" he exclaimed as he lowered his aching body into the foaming water, "This is the life, relaxing after a hard morning's work in a nice hot bath listening to my favourite music." And he drifted away in thoughts of what vegetables he would plant in his newly dug vegetable plot.

His thoughts were soon rudely interrupted, however, when all of a sudden the volume on the CD player went to maximum. Even in the bathroom the sound was overpowering and it immediately brought him back to reality.

"What is it with that player today?" He said angrily, and wrapping a towel around his dripping wet body went out to the CD player.

"That's odd," he remarked, "how could the volume change like that? The knob has to be pressed down hard."

Matt reset the volume control and resumed his soak but, once again, his bath time pleasure was to be interrupted. After just the first track the player once again stopped of its own accord.

"Sod it!" Shouted out Matt loudly, "Damn thing! Well, this time it can stay off. I'm not going out there again. I'm going to finish my bath in peace."

Soon afterwards Natalie came back with lots of shopping, "I'd almost forgotten what fun it was to go shopping but it's very tiring. Think I might have a bath rather than a shower."

"You do that. Hope it's better than mine," and Matt told Natalie about his earlier experience with the CD player.

"I've said for some time that you should get rid of that old player and get a more modern one."

"But how do you account for the player switching itself off and for the volume going up to maximum?"

"If it's not the machine then perhaps we've got a ghost," joked Natalie.

* * *

That night an exhausted Matt and Natalie went to bed early. About an hour after they fell asleep, however, they were rudely awakened by an almighty crash that resounded throughout the cottage.

"What on earth was that?" exclaimed Matt sitting bolt upright in bed.

"I have no idea, but it seemed to come from just outside the bedroom door," replied a very worried Natalie.

Very slowly and carefully they made their way onto the landing where, much to their surprise, they found that the hatch to the loft had opened and the loft ladder had crashed to the floor.

"Now that shouldn't happen," said Matt, "I've been up in that loft a few times and that loft hatch has a counter balancing weight to keep it in position; it should never come down on its own."

"Well, it did," said Natalie stating the obvious, "perhaps you didn't fasten it correctly."

"It doesn't matter. Even if the catch isn't fully engaged the counter weight should ensure it doesn't come open by itself. Still, let's worry about it in the morning I need to get back to sleep."

The next morning Matt closely examined the loft hatch but couldn't find any fault with the mechanism, "Must just be one of those things," he mused.

The incident with the loft hatch caused a certain amount of unease and Natalie, reflecting on the odd incidents that had happened since they moved into the cottage, asked, "You don't think we've got a ghost do you?"

"Certainly not," retorted Matt with hardly a thought, "I know this cottage is old but there's nothing to suggest it has ever been haunted or the scene of any murderous or nefarious goings-on."

"Come on then," urged Natalie, "give me a hand to move this furniture. I just want to move a couple of these chairs around so that we have more room going in and out of the kitchen."

A week later, however, Matt once again found himself being woken most roughly by his wife, "Matt, get up and come downstairs right now!"

"What is it this time," he said as he reluctantly got out of bed and followed Natalie down the stairs.

"Look! Look at that furniture!"

"What's the matter with it?"

"What's the matter with it?" retorted Natalie, "Just look at it. It's been moved. I came down to get breakfast ready and the first thing I saw was that the furniture had been moved back to how it was when we first came into the cottage! Matt I'm scared. What's happening in this house?"

"It's only a couple of chairs," Matt replied rather sheepishly, "Nothing to worry about. Are you sure you didn't move them back again?"

"Completely sure! This place is beginning to give me the creeps. I don't feel safe in here anymore."

"Look, if there was anything to worry about in this cottage then I'm sure John next door would have told us. After all, he did show us around when we first came to the village house hunting, and he could have mentioned it then."

"I suppose you're right. It could just be my imagination working overtime," and Natalie returned to the kitchen to prepare the breakfast.

* * *

About two weeks later once again Matt was rudely awoken by his light-sleeping wife.

"Matt, get up! There are voices coming from the sitting room. I know it's not the radio because the plug is pulled out."

Reluctantly Matt sat up in bed and listened. There were indeed muffled voices once again coming from the sitting room. He slowly got out of bed and made his way carefully and very quietly down the stairs. This time, however, he did not take one of the swords with him. Natalie followed about three paces behind. They listened outside the sitting room door; there were definitely voices coming from within.

Suddenly, on the count of three, Matt and Natalie burst through the sitting room door and, much to their surprise, found the television set was switched on and showing a documentary.

"Not again," said a very frustrated Natalie, "What is it about the appliances in this house? Can't they ever stay switched off? I distinctly remember turning that set off last thing before I came up to bed."

"You couldn't be mistaken?"

"Certainly not!" and without a further word Natalie switched the television off and violently pulled the plug from its socket, "There, that's fixed that! Come on, I've had enough of this, let's get back to bed."

Back in the bedroom Matt was musing out loud, "It is strange all these appliances switching themselves on and off. Do you remember when we first came here the television would sometimes switch off when we were watching it but that stopped after a couple of weeks. Then there was the washing machine, stopping in mid-cycle, but that seemed to fix itself after a couple of weeks. Luckily the fridge and the freezer never switched themselves off. Perhaps it's us, perhaps everything here just needs to get used to new owners; perhaps the cottage just doesn't like change."

"Maybe," agreed Natalie, "but there's no harm done so let's get back to sleep."

* * *

A few weeks later Natalie had some surprising news for Matt.

"Matt, I have something to tell you, I think I'm pregnant. I've missed my last two periods and I've just got a positive result from this pregnancy testing kit I picked up in Colchester yesterday."

"Really!" replied Matt with a broad smile as he grabbed hold of Natalie, kissed her on the lips, lifted her up and spun her round.

"Well you can stop spinning me round and be a bit more careful as this is definitely not good for the baby," retorted Natalie.

"I wonder what it will be, a boy or a girl?" Matt mused as he put Natalie firmly on the floor.

"I don't know but does it matter?"

"No, not at all; so long as it's healthy."

"That's the main thing. I suppose I'll have to make an appointment with the doctor. I can't say I'm looking forward to all those hospital visits, the tests and scans, midwives poking me about and all that stuff."

"Well, I'll be reassured that they're keeping a close eye on you. This will take some getting used to and will completely change our lives."

"And we've now got a use for that empty bedroom; we'll turn it into a nursery. Didn't John mention that the

Owens used that room as a nursery? We'll have a free hand to decorate and design it just as we want to. We can get a nice set of baby furniture with matching curtains, carpets and bedding. Perhaps we'll get something ultra modern as a contrast to the rest of the cottage."

"Don't get carried away," implored Matt, "we're not made of money. Still, you and the baby do deserve the best."

* * *

Almost seven months later Natalie was at home when her contractions began. She phoned the hospital then Matt drove her to the maternity unit rather than calling an ambulance.

"This baby must take after you," joked Natalie, "it has no patience, it can't wait!"

"Maybe," replied Matt as they approached the reception desk.

"Mr & Mrs Clutterbuck welcome, we've been expecting you since you telephoned. The orderly here will take you to your ward."

"Do I really have to be in a wheelchair? I'm perfectly capable of walking."

"Better to be safe than sorry," insisted the orderly, so Natalie reluctantly sat in the wheelchair.

"Please make yourself comfortable on the bed. The midwife will be here shortly. How are the contractions going?"

"They're becoming more frequent. I don't think it'll be long now."

"Well, you're in luck today, as the birthing suite is empty at the moment and we have two midwives on duty and a doctor," replied the nurse as Natalie lowered herself onto the bed with obvious discomfort, "Just waiting for you."

No sooner had Natalie stretched out on the bed when her waters broke. Immediately the nurse called for the midwife and an orderly and, turning to Matt, said, "Don't just stand here. Go with your wife. I take it you do want to be present for the birth?"

Matt quickly composed himself and followed the fast disappearing wheelchair. In no time at all he had reached the birthing suite and found himself dressed in a gown and face-mask and holding Natalie's hand as she listened to advice from the midwife. Without warning the contractions intensified and she began to give birth.

"Push!" shouted the midwife, "Push! You're doing very well. I can see the head so not long to go now."

After about 15 minutes it was all over and Natalie had given birth to a little girl. The midwife showed the baby to Natalie, who was by now exhausted, and then handed her to the doctor. The doctor examined the child, wrapped it in a blanket, and walked over to Matt.

As he put the baby in Matt's outstretched arms, he said in a whispered voice, "Mr Clutterbuck, I don't want to alarm you unnecessarily but the baby has a slight deformity. It's nothing serious and can quite easily be remedied."

Matt looked at the baby and said, "Yes, I can see that her eyes are different colours; one is greenish and the other is blue."

"That's no problem, the eyes should be the same colour by the time she starts secondary school."

"Then what is the problem doctor?"

"It's her feet; she has six toes on each foot. As I said, it's not a major problem, and we can amputate the extra toes once she is a few months old. Matter of fact, a surprising number of babies are born with extra appendages and it's quite a routine procedure to remove them."

"I'm not so sure, doctor, I don't see any harm in the extra toes and I wouldn't want to put her through any unnecessary pain and suffering."

"Oh, there won't be any pain involved. The operation takes place under a full general anaesthetic so she won't feel a thing."

"I'll discuss it with Natalie when she's recovered and we'll let you know our decision," and Matt walked over to Natalie and handed her the baby. Natalie eagerly clutched the baby close to her and closed her eyes in contentment.

Natalie remained in hospital for three days until the medical staff were satisfied that she and the baby were fit to go home. In that time Natalie had quickly come to terms with the baby's additional toes and agreed with Matt that they shouldn't be amputated. They named the baby Ruby after Natalie's grandmother.

The birth of a new baby generated a lot of excitement in Long Hooton but, after a few weeks, the number of visitors to the cottage diminished and things soon settled down into a routine for the new family. Even Matt resigned himself to some months of sleepless nights. This time, however, the sleepless nights weren't because of the television or radio coming on at night but caused by Ruby waking up and demanding to be fed. He remarked, partially in jest, that since Ruby had come to the cottage all the incidents of things switching themselves on and off had ceased.

* * *

It was coming up to Ruby's first birthday and she and the family were playing in the garden when John Brooksbank put his head over the ancient brick wall, "Nice to see young people having a good time and enjoying the weather. It's a pity we haven't more young people here in Long Hooton. By the way, my sister's staying with me for a couple of weeks and she was wondering if she could come over and meet the new arrival. Well, Ruby's not quite so new nowadays, of course, is she?"

"Of course she can," agreed Natalie, "We haven't met your sister before so it will be nice to get acquainted."

"I haven't mentioned this before but Cherry, that's my sister, lived with me for a while after her husband died but moved away about three months before you came to the village. You'll like her, she's a real bundle of fun."

"Come over anytime after 3 o'clock and we'll have tea and cakes out here in the garden. Natalie's been baking."

"That sounds fine to me," and John disappeared behind the wall.

Later that afternoon, John and Cherry let themselves through the small wrought-iron side gate into Wishing Well Cottage, and were soon sitting in the garden deep in conversation with Matt and Natalie.

"Where's Ruby," enquired Cherry after a little while, "I can't wait to see her. It's nice to have a baby back in the old cottage again."

"She's due to wake up shortly so I'll go and see how she is," said Natalie not picking up on Cherry's remarks and going inside the cottage.

"Here we are," announced Natalie proudly on her return, "Ruby's awake and couldn't wait to come and see who is in the garden. We need to keep a close eye on her because although she can't yet walk she can crawl and you'd be amazed at how quickly she can disappear."

After about half an hour of playing and making a fuss of the baby Cherry picked Ruby up in her arms and stared intensely at her face.

"I do believe she's got two different coloured eyes, one green and one blue. How extraordinary!"

"Well the doctors said it's not that uncommon and will correct itself," responded Natalie slightly on the defensive, "probably by the time she starts senior school."

"When I said extraordinary I didn't mean the colour of the eyes I meant how extraordinary that two little girls in the same cottage should have identical eyes."

"Two little girls?" enquired a rather bemused Natalie, "I don't understand."

"I'm talking about Melodie. Didn't John mention little Melodie? Melodie Owen, the daughter of the previous owners, she had different coloured eyes exactly like Ruby."

"How odd is that," remarked Matt who had just picked up on the conversation, "I had no idea the Owens had any children. There was no indication when we first looked round the cottage. Come to think about it there weren't any photographs here at all."

"That's because little Melodie died in the most tragic of circumstances and was the principal reason why the Owens moved back to London; they were devastated by her death. The poor little mite was only six years old at the time."

"We had no idea," acknowledged Natalie rather sorrowfully.

"Melodie was a lovely child and I enjoyed her company immensely. She was extremely well-mannered and polite and very advanced for her young years. She was fun to be with and also liked playing practical jokes. She would often hide the remote controls and when her parents weren't looking would switch things on and off. She didn't seem to like change so if her parents moved anything or had alterations made she would often creep downstairs at night and change them back to how they were before. I recall she even got into the loft on one occasion and tried to close the hatch from the inside but over-balanced and fell through. Luckily she wasn't hurt."

"So what happened to her?" asked an intrigued Natalie.

"It was tragic; she drowned in the wishing well! Her parents had forbidden her to go near the well and had boarded over the top but, somehow, she had managed to remove the boards. It is thought she peered over the top, lost her balance, and fell in. As you know the water is a long way down and by the time her parents realised she was missing and where she was it was too late; she had drowned. It was a terrible time for the whole village as Melodie was such a popular child. The Owens did try to get the well removed but this is a listed building and permission was refused. As I said, it wasn't long after that terrible incident that the Owens put the cottage on the market and moved away from the village."

"A sorry tale indeed," remarked Natalie as she took Ruby from Cherry and held her very tightly, "I would hate anything like that to happen to Ruby. We must put some kind of a lock on top of that well so the boards can't be removed easily."

"I always thought Melodie was special," Cherry continued, "and so did she. She was very proud of her different coloured eyes and she had something else that made her special too and of which she often boasted. You may find this hard to believe but she had six toes on each foot. Doctors had wanted to remove the extra digits but her parents were against it and Melodie enjoyed the attention this gave her. In a way it was her party piece and she never tired of showing people her extra toes."

Matt looked sheepishly at Natalie who instinctively cupped her hands over Ruby's feet but there was no need as the little girl was wearing ankle socks.

"Do you know?" enquired Cherry staring into Ruby's face, "I don't know whether or not it's the eyes, but there's more than a passing resemblance between little Ruby here and poor Melodie. In a way it's as if Melodie has come home. It's almost as if she's returned home to live in Wishing Well Cottage!"

The End

The events in this story were inspired by actual happenings which took place when the author and his wife moved into a bungalow in Witham, Essex. These happenings, however, ceased immediately upon the birth of their daughter.

The Gentleman Burglar

The Gentleman Burglar

"I'm sure the estate agent said we should drive right through the village and we'd find it on the left," said Elaine, trying to glance at both the map and the satnav at the same time as the cottages lining the road began to give way to open country and fields.

"You're right," replied Greg as he turned into Regency Grove, "we've arrived," and he parked the car outside one of the six houses making up this small, but exclusive, cul-de-sac.

"Very impressive!" exclaimed Elaine as she stared at the large Georgian-style villas in front of them, "They look huge from the outside. I can't wait to have a look at the inside."

Greg and Elaine, each clutching a portfolio of papers, got out of the car and strode up to a young snappily dressed man sitting by the front door of one of the houses.

"Mr and Mrs Smithson, glad you found it all right. I'm Matthew Wells from 'Country Houses of Distinction' and I'd like to welcome you to Regency Grove. Let's go inside," and he unlocked the front door and beckoned them to follow him inside.

"As I said when we spoke about this property earlier houses such as this do not come on the market very often. This is a select development of six individually styled Georgian houses that is just over three years old. Situated on the edge of the village and bordering on green belt land that cannot be developed. These are properties for the discerning connoisseur and built to the highest specifications."

"Wow! Look at this kitchen," and Elaine immediately marvelled at the ultra modern design and built-in appliances, "It's big enough to take a table and six chairs and it's even got a walk-in pantry!"

"That's not all," added Matthew taking full advantage of Elaine's enthusiasm, "there's a laundry room and utility room as well. The rest of the ground floor consists of a drawing room, dining room, sitting room, study and a ground floor cloakroom that also has a shower. Oh, and I almost forgot, there's a conservatory that runs the whole length of the drawing room. Come on, I'll show you around," and he led the way.

"At the top of these stairs we have the five bedrooms, three of which have en-suite bathrooms and there is, of course, a family bathroom with a Jacuzzi bath and a separate power shower," and he left Greg and Elaine to wander round the upstairs by themselves.

"The size of this bedroom and the en-suite," mused Elaine as she examined the double-size bath and the separate shower, "There's even individual 'his and hers' sinks – how's that for luxury?"

"It seems to have everything we're looking for," responded Greg, "have you noticed...."

"You bet," retorted Elaine, "three steps leading up to a sunken bath, granite and marble floor tiles and, if I'm not mistaken, those wall tiles and the frieze are Versace. This could be just the house for us."

"I think you're right. The double garage would also be ideal for our cars; no need to have one of them on the drive," and he followed his wife and Matthew down the stairs into the hall.

"If we make an offer how soon could we move in?"

"You're in luck. The current owners have had to move overseas at short notice as they've been posted to Australia. They've decided that as they'll be retiring in four or five years' time they'll stay there and not return to England."

"That's the reverse situation to what we find ourselves in," volunteered Greg, "I've been working in the States for the last ten years but my job now brings me back to the UK. How soon do you think we could complete the purchase?"

"On the basis that there'll be no chain and you're a cash buyer with no property to sell, you could be moving in within two or three weeks. Obviously you'll want to have a survey done but these properties were built to very exacting standards so I don't think you'll find any problems."

"That's fine," replied Greg with a smile on his face, "we'll call in your office tomorrow morning to sort out the paperwork," and after shaking Matthew's hand he and Elaine walked out of the house arm in arm with a noticeable spring in their step.

"See you tomorrow," shouted Matthew as he took the keys out of his pocket and locked the heavy oak front door.

* * *

"Am I glad that's the last of them," sighed Elaine as the large delivery lorry snaked its way out of Regency Grove, "perhaps we can now have a bit of peace and quiet to decide where we'll put everything."

"I thought you'd already done that," joked Greg as he flopped down on one of the brand new sofas, "but I must say it is rather nice to be surrounded by all this new furniture. In a way it's a new beginning for us. Hopefully we'll be able to settle down here. I'm tired of our former nomadic way of life."

"I agree, but working for Smith, Beyer and Benson in America for all those years did set us up rather nicely from a financial point of view. This house is everything I've dreamed about. I think we're going to be very happy here."

"Let's celebrate. We're both tired from taking deliveries all day and moving stuff around. I suggest we have an early night. What do you say we try out that large bath? I'll put a bottle of champagne on ice – we can have a relaxing soak together and a drink at the same time."

"That sounds fine to me. I need to unwind and get a good night's sleep."

"Great, I'll just go and …." But Greg's words were cut short by the sound of the front door bell. "Blast!" he exclaimed, "I wonder who that can be? You stay here I'll go and see who it is," and he reluctantly forced himself up from the sofa and made his way to the front door.

"Hello, sorry to disturb you on your first day here but my wife asked me to pop over and see if there is anything you need."

"Well, that's very kind of you Mr…."

"Hillman, John Hillman, I live across the way at number six."

"Greg, Greg Smithson, pleased to meet you," and he shook hands warmly with John Hilllman. "At the moment I think we have everything under control but please come in and meet my wife, Elaine."

"No, I'd better not. I can appreciate how tired you both must be. However, there is an ulterior motive to my coming over. On Saturday week we're having one of our twice-yearly dinner parties and everybody in the Grove is invited. It's a rare chance for us all to come together. For most of the time the members of our small community here hardly see each other. It will also give you and your wife the opportunity to meet us and see what you've let yourselves in for. What do you say?"

"It's very kind of you. We'll be delighted to come."

"Fine, see you at seven-thirty. Don't be late, everyone will be dying to meet you," and John left with a big smile on his face.

Greg returned to the drawing room and told Elaine about the invitation to the dinner party.

"I'll have to buy a new dress!"

"What nonsense! You've got plenty of suitable dresses."

"I certainly have not! I gave most of my clothes away to charity before we left the States. Travel light you said. Hope a week and a day is long enough to find something appropriate."

"You'll manage," said Greg playfully, "Come on let's grab some champagne and get in that bath!"

* * *

"Greg! Elaine! Come on in and meet the gang; they're all here. We like to think we're part of a family," and John ushered the couple into the drawing room.

"I must say," said John admiring Elaine's dress, "you look stunning in that outfit. You're a very lucky man Greg."

The room was buzzing with the sound of countless conversations but the atmosphere became hushed as Greg and Elaine entered the room.

"Silence everyone," boomed John in his rather authoritative voice, "I'd like to introduce you to our new neighbours, let's welcome them as our new friends, Greg and Elaine," and everybody turned to look at the newcomers.

"I'm Jackie, John's wife," said a rather petite individual who walked forward with a drink in her hand, "Help yourselves to a drink then we'll go into the dining room. The meal's almost ready. Follow me."

"Here, sit at this end of the table next to me. You'll then get a better view of who's who," piped up John, and he pulled out a chair for Elaine.

Elaine looked around the table. "Glad I bought that expensive dress," she thought to herself, "Although they all look as if they're in their fifties, like Greg and me, I've never seen so many designer outfits in one place before in my life. It was never like this in the States. And all that jewellery; I knew I should have worn more gold, but these people seem to be dripping in diamonds as well!"

Then, much to Elaine's surprise, uniformed waiters appeared and began to serve the food.

"So much easier than cooking it yourself," said a smiling Jackie as if she was reading Elaine's thoughts.

"Quite," stammered Elaine.

John poured a glass of wine and then announced, "Time for us to get acquainted. I'm sure Greg and Elaine want to know what they've let themselves in for by moving here. I'll kick off first. First of all I don't want to be considered a chauvinist but let's face it none of the ladies around this table work; it's us men that are the breadwinners."

"And quite right too," interjected Jackie, "we're all too busy doing things in the village. We're on all sorts of committees and, before you interrupt John, yes we do enjoy the odd day out in town engaging in a bit of retail therapy."

"Suits me fine," smiled Elaine, "Since we went to the States I've not worked either. My philosophy is to support my husband in whatever he does, both on the work front and on the social scene."

"I think you're going to fit in here just fine," Jackie agreed, "Our kind of people."

"Let's get the formal bit over and done with," suggested John, "On your left Elaine are Stuart and Katie Blackburn."

"Pleased to meet you," said Stuart, "I'm not into anything as exciting as John. For my sins I'm an

Investment Manager at Courts and deGroot International Bankers in the City. Afraid I'm the dull one around here."

"Still, if you want any investment advice, then Stuart's your man," added John enthusiastically, "he's made a few bob for me now and again. Well worth having a chat with him sometime. On Stuart's left are Tony and Marion Broadway. Tony made his pile in DIY."

"That's right," Tony said emptying his glass, "Pleased to meet you by the way. Yes, I got into the home improvement market in the boom years of the eighties and ended up owning a chain of wholesale builders' merchants. Anything you want doing in the building line then I can introduce you to reliable tradesmen and rock-bottom prices."

"On Tony and Marion's left are Barry and Marilyn Linsell. They add a bit of culture to Regency Grove," teased John.

"Don't you believe it," acknowledged Barry, "What John means to say is that I'm the arts and theatre critic for the BBC. I also review books and CDs for the Times Newspapers for my sins."

"Finally," said John, "we have Richard and Pat Hallwood. Richard's our technical whiz on all things to do with IT."

"John's too kind. I'm the Head of IT Development at Microsoft UK. The title sounds much more impressive than what the work actually entails. Usually I'm reduced to sorting out problems with my family's PCs."

"What about you John?" enquired Greg, "You haven't told us what you do for a living."

"Back to reality," sighed John, "I used to be an Assistant Commissioner with the Metropolitan Police but I retired a few years ago and now I head security for BAA."

"Nice to know we're in safe hands then," said Greg raising his glass.

"I wouldn't say that," joked Richard, "you haven't caught the 'Gentleman Burglar' yet."

"The Gentleman Burglar?" responded a puzzled looking Greg.

"The one that got away!" teased Stuart.

"I suppose you'd find out sooner or later," added Jackie, "Perhaps you'd better tell him John."

Reluctantly John put his glass on the table, "There really is very little crime in this village let alone this small cul-de-sac but all of us here have fallen victim to an intruder we've nicknamed the 'Gentleman Burglar'. He seems to know a lot about us and when we are out and that is when he strikes. He never leaves any clues and takes only small things of very high value."

"Someone local then?" suggested Elaine.

"Could be," acknowledged John, "we even thought it could be one of us but then, when you look around, none of us in these six houses are in need of the money."

"Somebody could be doing it for the sheer thrill and excitement then? These things do happen," chipped in Greg.

"No, that only happens in fiction, not real life."

"So why do you call him the Gentleman Burglar?" enquired Greg looking straight at John.

"Simple, unlike most intruders he is most particular. He takes only the most valuable items and goes to great pains not to make a mess and to leave everything as it was when he entered the house. Often it is some days before we discover he has paid us a visit. Of course we've had the police investigate but so far they've been unable to come up with even the smallest clue as to his identity."

"Well, the estate agent didn't tell us about that," said a worried looking Elaine.

"He wouldn't," said John, "we've never gone public. Each of us here owns lots of very valuable items and things which are very precious to us and we feel that if we give this burglar any sort of publicity then it could alert others to come into the area and copy his example."

"We'll take heed and make sure that whenever we're away or out of the house the burglar alarm is always switched on," said Greg.

"You do that," responded Barry, "but a burglar alarm didn't stop him stealing my collection of rare Victorian automata."

"I've got something else that may deter him," mused Greg.

"What's that?" asked Richard enthusiastically, "Some sort of electronic wizardry or computer software?"

"Perhaps it's some sort of a trap?" enquired Tony.

"Nothing so exciting, I'm afraid," admitted Greg, "What I've got in mind is something to build on his reputation for not leaving a mess."

"I'm intrigued now," added Marilyn, "do let us into your secret."

"Call it extra insurance if you like," Greg replied with a hint of mischief in his voice, "I've got a cellar of very fine wines so, if we go away for a few days, then I'm going to leave him a bottle of wine."

"A bottle of wine!" exclaimed Kate, "You're going to give a burglar a bottle of wine for breaking into your house!"

"Not exactly. When we go away I'll leave a bottle of wine, and a very good vintage at that, on a table in the hall together with a glass. The 'Gentleman Burglar', if he does decide to pay us a visit will, hopefully, appreciate the gesture and be even more careful and not do any unnecessary damage."

"Well, let's hope it won't come to that," reassured John, "He hasn't been in evidence much lately. Are you thinking of going away in the near future?"

"Not for a couple of months. We've booked a three-week cruise from Barbados that sails up the Amazon. Thought we'd relax a bit after the turmoil of coming back from America and setting up a new home."

"Sounds an excellent idea to me," remarked Stuart, "wish we were going with you."

After the meal drinks were served in the drawing room and the dinner party eventually finished at about two in the morning.

"Thank goodness it's Saturday and you don't have to go to work tomorrow, darling," Elaine managed to say between yawns as she and Greg almost fell through their front door, "Nice people. I think I'm going to like living here."

"Yes," agreed Greg, "very genuine and sincere people. I did wonder before we met them what they'd be like. Sometimes people with such obvious wealth and influence can tend to be somewhat aloof but I didn't detect any such trait amongst them."

"Quite the contrary, I found them to be very down to earth. As you said, we're going to like living here."

"What about that burglar though? Do you think we should be worried?"

"Well the others didn't seem too worried so why should it worry us. I'm sure we can deal with this so called 'Gentleman Burglar'. Come on, let's get up to bed, I'm worn out. Besides, it's Sunday morning already!"

* * *

"Come on Elaine, do hurry up, the taxi will be here any minute now!"

"Don't worry I'll be ready, there's plenty of time. After all, the reason we're staying at a hotel near the airport tonight is so we won't have to worry about missing our plane in the morning. So, no real panic, I'm sure the taxi driver won't mind waiting a little while for us."

"I like the idea of the hotel stay, it means the holiday starts a day earlier and we get to the airport refreshed. That journey along the motorway with all that traffic is a terrible way to start the holiday. It can put us in a bad mood if we're worried about getting to the airport on time and not missing our flight."

Greg struggled to get the cases down the stairs and just as he put them down in the hall the door bell rang.

"I'll get it darling. Once the bags are in the taxi I'll have another look round the house to double check everything is locked and the burglar alarm is on."

"Fine, I'm on my way," and after a couple of minutes Elaine came down the stairs and got into the taxi.

Greg soon joined her and the taxi sped off towards the airport.

* * *

That very evening soon after midnight, a figure dressed all in black and wearing a face-mask, silently entered the Smithson's house. The figure walked through the kitchen and into the hall without a sound and his gaze immediately fell upon the bottle of wine. By the light of a small pocket torch he looked at the wine and after pouring out a glass removed his face mask to take a sip. It was none other than their neighbour Stuart Blackburn.

"I must say," thought Stuart to himself, "when Greg said he would leave out a really good vintage he wasn't kidding. This wine is absolutely divine, could almost drink a second glass! Perhaps I'll come back tomorrow night and have a good look round. There must be lots of things of value in here."

* * *

"I can't believe three weeks could go by so fast but here we are about to turn into Regency Grove," sighed

Elaine as she thought about their wonderful holiday, "I wonder if everything's all right at home?"

"Don't worry," reassured Greg, "I'm sure everything's fine and nothing has been taken. It'll take more than a so-called 'Gentleman Burglar' to get the better of me."

The taxi turned round on the drive and left Regency Grove. Greg unlocked the front door, lifted the cases into the hall, and was closely followed indoors by Elaine.

"Everything ok darling?" asked Elaine rather sheepishly expecting the worst and the house to be ransacked.

"Looks just as we left it," replied Greg reassuringly but then hesitated and added, "The wine's been opened. Look, that glass has been used," and holding the wine bottle up to the light added, "And someone's helped themselves to more than a few glasses of my wine!"

Elaine remained firmly rooted to the spot while Greg looked round the hall then carefully peered into all the downstairs rooms.

"I don't understand this," he said with a puzzled look on his face, "all the doors and windows are locked and nothing's been taken or even disturbed. Everything seems to be in order. You wait here and I'll check upstairs," and Greg cautiously ascended the stairs. Elaine stayed put for a few minutes then picked up the glass and bottle of wine and took them into the kitchen.

She rinsed out the glass and tipped the remains of the wine down the sink.

A few minutes later Greg appeared on the landing. He announced that all was well and nothing appeared to be missing.

"Very curious," mused Elaine, "very curious indeed. Why break into a house and not bother to steal anything? There are lots of things here that are easy to carry away and could be sold for a lot of money."

"I agree," concurred Greg, "very puzzling. Still, let's not dwell on the matter, let's just be grateful that the 'Gentleman Burglar' or whoever paid us a visit obviously thought there was nothing here to interest him. Come on it's getting late; let's have an early night and see how things look in the morning.

Elaine made sure the doors and windows were secure then joined her husband upstairs. They were very tired after their journey and soon they both fell deeply asleep.

* * *

Unusually for both Greg and Elaine they overslept and it was while having a late breakfast that there was a knock on the front door.

"I've only got my nightie on, you see who it is Greg and whoever it is don't let them in. I don't want anyone seeing me like this with my hair all the over the place and not even having washed."

"Ok darling," and Greg made his way to the front door.

"John! Richard!" exclaimed Greg in surprise at seeing two of his neighbours standing on his doorstep, "Shouldn't you two be at work?"

"Ordinarily yes," replied John with more than a degree of hesitation in his voice, "Look, can we come in, there's something you need to know and we don't want to talk about it on the doorstep."

"Of course," conceded Greg totally forgetting about Elaine's instruction, "Come through to the kitchen. We've only just got up and are having a late breakfast. Excuse the mess and the dressing gown."

"Or no dressing gown!" retorted Elaine, as Greg ushered John and Richard into the kitchen, seemingly totally oblivious to her predicament.

"Pull up a chair. Tea for anyone?" asked Greg.

"No thanks, it's not really a social call," remarked John rather coldly, "I'm afraid we've got some sad news to tell you, about Stuart."

"Stuart?"

"Yes," interjected Richard, "I'm afraid he's dead."

"Dead!" exclaimed Elaine, "He can't be. That's awful. How did it happen? Was it an accident?"

"No, he had a massive stroke. It was the day after you left on your holiday. He went to the office as normal but during the afternoon he was taken ill and rushed to hospital in London. Despite all the efforts of the doctors he didn't regain consciousness and died later that evening."

"That's unbelievable," murmured Elaine completely forgetting about her dishevelled appearance, "How's Kate taking it? She must be devastated."

"She certainly is," Richard said slowly, "but there's something else you should know. It turns out that Stuart wasn't the bank's Chief Investment Manager at all, he was just a low level clerk on an average salary. Goodness knows how he could afford to live in one of these houses and enjoy the lavish lifestyle he's led over the last few years. Kate is not only distraught at Stuart's death but also at finding out about their precarious financial position. It looks like she'll have to sell the house."

"That really is awful. Perhaps I should go round and see her," said Elaine, "and express our sympathy."

"Well that's partly why we've come round so early," interjected John, "Because of Stuart's sudden death and the fact that he was in hospital for less than 24 hours before he died there had to be a post-mortem. This delayed the release of the body and it didn't prove possible to arrange the funeral to take place until today."

"That's right," added Richard, "we thought you'd want to go to the funeral so we've reserved seats for you in our limousine. We leave at noon. Afterwards there are light refreshments at Kate's house. You can speak to her then as you may not get an opportunity at the crematorium."

"That's very good of you both," acknowledged Greg, "We'll get ready and be over at your house just before 12 o'clock."

"Fine," said John and Richard almost in unison and they left via the kitchen door.

"Who'd have thought it?" asked a clearly upset Elaine, "Looking at Stuart you would think he was the picture of health."

"Just shows," said Greg, "You never can tell when your time's up. One moment you're here and the next you're gone. Come on, we'd better get ready, don't want to be late."

* * *

After the funeral the neighbours in Regency Grove gathered in Kate's house together with Kate and Stuart's three children and a few other relatives. The atmosphere was initially sombre but, as is often the case at these wakes, the mood soon lightened up and the conversation quickly turned to more worldly matters. Inevitably amongst the women the subject of their husband's careers was raised.

"Tell me Elaine," enquired Pat who was obviously the worse for wear having drunk far too much wine,

"How's Greg settling down to life and work back in the UK?"

"Initially everything was fine but it now looks like he's going to be made redundant."

"Redundant!" repeated Pat emphasising every syllable, "Redundant!"

"Why's that," said a sympathetic sounding Marilyn, "I thought Smith, Beyer and Benson were market leaders in the pharmaceutical industry. Isn't there talk of a major new breakthrough with a new form of cancer drug? I'm sure I read that somewhere."

"That's quite right," acknowledged Elaine, "and I shouldn't really tell you this as much of Greg's work is secret, you know industrial spies and all that, but a major project he was working on has had to be abandoned. That's why he's going to be made redundant. He'll get a nice golden handshake that will allow us to continue with our present lifestyle but I know he'll miss the work."

"That is a shame," nodded Marilyn, "So what went wrong?"

"I don't really know the details but from what little Greg has told me it appears that this new cancer drug had remarkable results. All the tests were extremely positive and encouraging but, just as the drug was about to be launched, it became apparent that if a certain amount was taken then, instead of acting against the cancer, it had the effect of causing a stroke. Apparently no trace of the drug remained in the body and that was the reason it took so long for this awful effect to be discovered."

"Just as well it was discovered in time then. Think of the damage that would have resulted if the drug had actually been put into general use. Lots of people could have ended up just like poor old Stuart!"

"Yes, it doesn't bear thinking about, does it?" answered Elaine in a faltering voice as a sudden, terrible realisation shot through her mind as she looked over at her husband who was deep in conversation with Stuart's children. In a split second her mind was flooded with images; of Greg carefully selecting the bottle of wine, his insistence on placing it in a prominent position in the hall, and his remark that "No 'Gentleman Burglar' will get the better of me." Greg saw her glance at him and he raised a glass and, as she acknowledged the gesture, he winked and smiled knowingly.

The End

A Circle of Angels,
Deep in War

A Circle of Angels,
Deep in War

The three post-graduate students spilled out of the lift. Wrestling with their heavy backpacks they staggered down the short corridor into the university's half-empty restaurant. They quickly found a free table and stacked their luggage high on adjacent chairs.

"Well, we won't be back here again for some time," exclaimed Elaine, getting her breath back from her exertions.

"I can't believe it," added Natalie, "a couple of months' field work and then it's our final year."

"The end of what will be six long years of hard work," emphasised Michelle as she picked up a fallen bag, "but it'll be worth it to get decent well-paid jobs."

"I'll get the coffees," volunteered Natalie, and she made her way to the almost empty counter.

"Just making sure I've got everything; passport, tickets, etc.," said Elaine rummaging in her handbag as Natalie returned holding the three hot cups of coffee rather precariously between her outstretched hands.

"Very true," added Michelle as she gingerly sipped the very hot coffee.

"I still think I've drawn the short straw, though," sighed Elaine as she blew onto the coffee in a vain attempt to cool it down, "You're going to excavate in the gardens of Versailles," she said as she gave Michelle a disapproving glance, "and you're going to be digging around in the dungeons of a medieval castle in Prague," she added as Natalie gave her a big smile.

"It's tough," Michelle and Natalie added in unison and smiled, "but somebody's got to do it!"

"Tell me again," enquired Natalie somewhat rhetorically, "Just where exactly *are* you going?"

"You know very well where I'm going. You just want to gloat. You're both off to some very glamorous places and I'm going to the back of beyond. Well, Shetland, then."

"Digging around in some old convent isn't it?" giggled Michelle.

"You can laugh all you like but it might just be as rewarding as your digs. I've been doing a bit of research and it appears that on the small island I'm going to there was both a convent and a monastery. Apparently they existed side by side for hundreds of years but suddenly, in the sixteenth century, they were both abandoned and are now little more than ruins."

"A convent and a monastery," said Natalie somewhat playfully, "sounds like a recipe for some hanky-panky if you ask me. With all those nuns living next to all those monks! Who knows what might have gone on behind those thick stone walls."

"Nothing like that went on at all," Elaine quickly interjected, "it was common practice all over medieval Britain, and indeed before, for convents and monasteries to be built close to each other. There were even some instances of nuns and monks actually sharing the same buildings."

"Well, who knows what you might discover," said Natalie giving Elaine a knowing wink.

"Look at the time," reminded Michelle, "we're soon going to have to leave if we don't want to miss our trains."

"Yes, you're right," agreed Elaine, "but here's something to think about. You two are going to your digs by train and, do you realise, you'll get there before I do and I'm flying. Strange isn't it. I'm going to the very north of Britain and it'll take me longer than you two going to Europe."

"You do have a rather difficult journey, though," added Natalie.

"Yes," sighed Elaine, "I get the train from Liverpool Street to Stansted, take a plane to Aberdeen, then get a light aircraft to Lerwick and, finally, take the ferry to the island of Kirkgilda which I'd never even heard of before getting this dig. Good thing the university made all the arrangements. I just have to make sure I get to each segment of the journey on time."

The three friends then embraced and said their farewells, donned their oversized backpacks, and went their separate ways.

* * *

Elaine took the tube to Liverpool Street Station and emerged onto the very busy concourse.

"Why couldn't they have got me an earlier flight? It's right in the middle of the rush hour and just look at all these people," Elaine mumbled to herself as she looked at the sea of commuters engulfing the concourse while struggling to find the indicator board to learn which platform her train would leave from.

As she fought her way through the throng of commuters she was vaguely aware of some gypsy women to the front of her, trying to sell small bunches of white heather to the obviously disinterested mass of humanity, whose only thoughts were to get to their trains as quickly as possible. Indeed, the gypsy women were almost forcing the small bunches onto the unwary. She spied her platform and turned to try and get there in a straight line but, as she did so, she collided with one of the gypsy women.

"Lucky white heather, dearie?" the gypsy woman implored, and thrust a bunch of the flowers towards her. But, as the gypsy woman looked into Elaine's face, she recoiled as if she had seen a ghost and immediately turned to walk away.

"What's the matter?" snapped a surprised Elaine, "Don't you want me to buy your heather?"

"Beware the angels!" stammered the gypsy woman almost unable to find her words, "Beware the angels. A circle of angels, deep in war! Beware!" and she disappeared into the crowd.

"How strange," thought Elaine, "I wonder what she meant? Obviously deranged if you ask me," and without further thought she began to fight her way to her platform and awaiting train.

The train journey to Stansted went without incident and, much to her surprise, she arrived there in good time for her flight to Aberdeen. This was a very smooth flight and, when she arrived, the small aircraft for the final leg of her journey was already waiting for her on the tarmac. Less than an hour later she had landed near Lerwick and soon afterwards she arrived at the small hotel where she would spend the night. Even though it had gone 10:00 pm she was surprised to find that it was still quite light.

Elaine then sought out the hotel's small bar and surprised both the barman and the regulars when she tried a local brew that she couldn't obtain back home in England, Belhaven Best. In discussion with the locals she learned that the ferry to Kirkgilda left at 10:00 the next morning from the very end of the small quay and that it ran only once a week. Once on the island there was no easy way back and she was told just how remote the island was. Apart from the National Trust presence in the convent grounds, where she would be staying, there were just a few isolated farm houses but, other than that, it was just sheep, cattle and a few horses.

Despite sharing a few drinks with the locals she was unable to get them to talk much about the island apart from confirming that the convent and the monastery had both been in ruins for about five hundred years. They disclosed that several digs had been started over recent years but most had been quickly abandoned and nothing of significance had ever been found.

It was with a mixture of excitement and unease that Elaine lay on the bed in her small hotel room deep in thought before she eventually drifted off to sleep. She slept soundly and got up for an early breakfast and a quick walk around the town before making her way to the quay in search of the ferry. As she rounded the end of the quay she came to a stop and, with a puzzled look on her face, asked a man in a small boat where the ferry to Kirkgilda left from.

"You've found it," was the reply, "this is the ferry to Kirkgilda!"

"But this is such a small boat. You've only got room for four or five passengers at best. And I thought the journey to Kirkgilda took three hours."

"That's right it does, and this is the ferry. Not what you were expecting I'm sure, but she's a good boat and will get us there safe and sound," the boatman replied with a wry smile, "providing we don't get any rough seas," he added rather disparagingly.

Elaine climbed down into the small boat clutching her backpack and hand luggage as best she could. She eased herself into one of the seats and plonked her luggage down to the side of her hoping it would stay dry on the semi open deck.

"I'm Donald McDonald," said the boatman, and offered Elaine his hand.

"Pleased to meet you Donald; I'm Elaine Stuart," she replied shaking his hand warmly.

"Stuart! That's a good old Scottish name."

"Well, this is the first time I've ever been to Scotland."

"That's a pity. You could have chosen a better place for your first visit, but no matter," and Donald cast off.

"What about the other passengers?" enquired Elaine.

"Other passengers?" grinned Donald, "There aren't any. You're the only one today and most likely the only one this month. Hold tight! It can be a little choppy until we clear the harbour," and he steered the small boat out into the open sea.

* * *

After an hour, during which neither of them made any significant conversation, Donald volunteered, "We're making good time as we're going with the current and are about half way there now," and he pointed to what looked like a speck on the horizon.

Elaine looked towards the back of the boat and saw Mainland sink below the horizon. She looked forward and could just make out the shape of a craggy island coming into view.

"How long did you say you'll be staying on Kirkgilda?"

"Two months," replied Elaine, "unless we finish our excavations sooner."

"Rather you than me. I'd never spend a single night on that island let alone two months. I've been ferrying people to Kirkgilda for nearly 50 years and have never spent more than an hour there."

"Why's that?" enquired a curious Elaine, "Is the place haunted?"

"Not exactly. But there are lots of tales of spooky goings on and unexplained disappearances and the like. I don't believe them myself, you understand, but I'd rather not take a chance. My father, Donald, felt the same. He did this job before me and he never spent a night on the island either."

Elaine couldn't help a wry smile, "Your father was called Donald?"

"That's right, and his father before him, and his father before him. I'm one of a long line of Donald McDonalds and very proud of it. We're well known in these parts and can trace our ancestry back well over 500 years to when these islands were owned by the Danes."

"Very impressive," nodded Elaine, as she looked closely at the rather forbidding and barren landscape coming into view as the boat fast approached the island.

Some time later Donald brought the boat gently alongside a small wooden jetty and tied her up at the base of some well-rusted wrought iron stairs that led up the almost sheer cliff face.

"Here," he said, "I'll help you carry your things up to the top," and before Elaine could stop him the much older man had scooped up her rucksack and bags and almost ran up the hundred or so metal steps to the cliff top.

A visibly out of breath Elaine eventually joined him at the top.

"Follow this track over that hill and you'll see the convent of St. Gilda a few hundred yards in front of you. It'll be a bit misty up there today but it's the first of the two ruins, you can't miss it. The other building about half a mile behind it is the monastery of St. Gregory. I hope you enjoy your stay. Now I really must be going," and Donald almost tripped over in his haste to get back to his boat.

"Wait a minute," and Elaine reached into her purse.

"No need for that, my dear," said Donald politely refusing the tip, "your fare has been paid by the university and I couldn't take anything from someone going to the convent. You keep your money, I have a feeling you may be in need of it," and, without a further word, he returned to the metal stairs and began the long climb down to the jetty.

Elaine was surprised, and thought to herself, somewhat out of character, but reflecting the traditional English view of the Scots, "A Scotsman who refused a tip, who didn't want to take my money, now there's a first!" She then shrugged her shoulders, placed the heavy pack on her back, picked up her other bags and started out along the rather uneven and partly overgrown track up the hill.

* * *

By the time she reached the summit of the small hill Elaine was clearly tiring under the weight of her baggage and the steep uphill climb.

"I must spend more time in the gym next year. I'm getting out of condition. Perhaps I'll get time to explore the island once I've settled in and go for a few long jogs along the coast. I'm the last of our little group to arrive so, hopefully, they'll have got the programme for the dig organised by now," and she looked down into the valley.

"That's strange," she said out aloud, "I can see both the convent and the monastery through the mist and they both look to be in good condition, they don't look like ruins at all," and she began the long trudge down the slope towards the convent.

Nearly an hour after leaving the boat she walked through the open gates of the convent and made her way to the main entrance. As she did so she was amazed at the gardens and the variety of vegetables and fruit being grown there. "I bet they're almost self-sufficient here and could easily withstand being cut off from the other islands," she mused as she pulled sharply on the rope by the side of the heavy wooden doors and heard the chime of a distant bell inside.

After a little while the door creaked and slowly opened but, instead of one of the team she was expecting to meet, the person standing in front of Elaine was clearly a nun and dressed in what could only be described as a very old-fashioned nun's habit, which concealed most of her body.

"I'm sorry," blurted Elaine, "I didn't realize the convent was still in use. I thought it had been abandoned long ago."

"Whatever gave you that idea, child?" the nun said very quietly and deliberately, "We've been here for over 500 years and we've no intention of going anywhere. Please come in, I'm sure the Abbess will want to meet you and introduce you to the members of our order."

Elaine entered the building. She looked around her and was surprised at the apparent good order of the building. Admittedly it was somewhat sparsely furnished, mainly bare stone walls with a minimum of tapestries and wall coverings, but it had an air of contemplation and serenity about it. Perhaps this was partly due to the heavy smell of incense which hung in the air and seemed to pervade the very fabric of the building itself.

"The Abbess is busy right now but I'll show you to your cell. I'm Sister Astrid by the way."

"Cell!" thought Elaine to herself, but then quickly remembered that this was what the nuns' rooms in a convent were called. Perhaps the other members of the team had also been assigned cells so they could actually experience what life was like in the convent all those years ago. Struggling with her baggage she followed Sister Astrid along the dark corridors wondering why the professor or any other member of the team hadn't come to greet her.

"Here you are," said Sister Astrid opening a heavy wooden door, "this is your cell for as long as you stay with us."

Elaine looked around, "A bit basic isn't it!" she exclaimed, "There's just a wooden table and a chair. And that bed is nothing more than a heap of straw in a wooden frame. By the way, where's the light? You can't expect me to work just by the light of those candles can you?"

"Why not!" Sister Astrid retorted, "We do, it's perfectly adequate for us to study our texts, meditate and contemplate our faith. What more do we need?"

"If you say so," replied a bemused Elaine, "and where's the washing facilities and the toilet?"

"There's a bowl and a jug of water over there in that corner by the window," Sister Astrid said pointing towards a high barred window, "and you can relieve yourself behind that screen."

Elaine peered behind the screen to find a wooden bucket and a pile of straw.

"Now look here!" she protested, "This so-called realism is all fine and good but I do like to have proper washing and showering facilities, this simply will not do. Come on, the joke's over. Where's my real room?"

"I've made it clear that this is your cell. This is where you will be staying. If you don't like it then take the matter up with the Abbess when she sends for you," and without another word Sister Astrid turned and rather indignantly left the room.

Elaine sat and pondered the situation and after some time had passed came to a decision, "If the professor and the other students won't come to me then I'll go and find them," and she got up and peered out of the cell door.

The long corridor was empty and Elaine slowly walked along it looking into some of the other cells,

"Well these cells certainly seem occupied. There are plenty of old-looking manuscripts and some really ancient bibles in these rooms but just look at the clothes!" she exclaimed to herself, "Apart from some nuns' habits there are just what look like a few rags."

At the end of the corridor she came to a set of stone steps leading down a spiral staircase into what she took to be the convent's cellars. She was on the verge of returning to her cell when she heard the faint sounds of chanting.

"That sounds like some sort of prayer or incantation. It must be the professor and the team re-enacting some sort of ancient ritual. It would be just like him to try and evoke the atmosphere of this place," and Elaine slowly descended the steps which were very poorly lit by large candles placed at intervals in small alcoves. She reached the bottom and edged down a dimly lit passageway towards the sound of the voices and, as she looked into a large cavernous hall, she almost let out a scream. In the middle of the hall was a large altar and a young man was strapped naked and spread-eagled to it. Chanting and processing round the altar in an anti-clockwise direction was a group of women wearing nothing but the flimsiest of full-length see-through white negligees. Each woman was wielding a large knife and, as she looked, Elaine saw that Sister Astrid was amongst them.

Elaine looked on in sheer disbelief as the chanting became both louder and faster and the women got closer and closer to the altar brandishing their knives.

Suddenly they stopped and flung themselves to the ground prostrating before a huge wooden cross with a crucified figure on it. Elaine looked at the cross and gulped; the figure nailed to it was in the familiar position but, instead of a male figure, the cross sported a half-naked female figure.

Huge bowls of incense billowed out their intoxicating fragrances and as Elaine struggled to see through the encroaching mist the women rose up naked and started to encircle the altar once again. This time the chanting was led by a woman in a long purple negligee who appeared to be the leader and, on her command, the others came to an abrupt halt surrounding the altar. The male figure strapped to the altar was struggling and screaming but to no avail as the women seemed totally oblivious to his cries. Suddenly the woman in the purple negligee raised her knife and the others followed suit. They held this position for what seemed an eternity and then, entirely in unison, they plunged their knives into the body of the young man tied to the altar.

Elaine screamed and passed out.

* * *

Elaine woke up and found she was lying on the straw mattress in her cell. She looked around and standing before her was Sister Astrid and another woman both of whom were wearing nuns' habits.

"You must have fallen asleep," said Sister Astrid in hushed tones, "so the Abbess decided to pay you a visit."

Elaine immediately recognised the Abbess as the woman she had seen in the basement dressed in the long purple negligee. She had led the others in murdering the young man strapped to the altar. But could this really be happening? Was this possible? She reasoned with herself that in this day and age these things just did not go on. They were confined to the darker pages of history. Still, where were the professor and the student team? And that figure on the cross! She knew that in the first century or so after the birth of Christ there were many weird sects, some of them heretical, but she had never heard of any that worshipped a female Christ. All these thoughts flashed through her mind in an instant.

"Sister Astrid tells me you are tired after your journey. You must have fallen asleep," suggested the Abbess.

"But the basement! That poor man on the altar!" stammered Elaine, "It was all so real and where is the professor and the others?"

"What strange fantasies and words you are saying," replied the Abbess rather condescendingly, "but I'm sure you'll feel better in the morning after a good night's sleep. I'll look in on you in the morning myself," and the Abbess left the room.

"Sister Hilda, our Abbess, is concerned about you. We all are," Sister Astrid tried to reassure Elaine, "Here, I've brought you something to eat. I'll fetch you in the morning and take you to breakfast in the Great Hall where you can meet the other Sisters," and Sister Astrid placed a metal plate with some bread and water on it on the table in front of Elaine and left the cell, locking it after her.

Elaine stared at the hunk of brown, almost black, bread which looked most unappetising and slowly lifted it to her mouth. She hadn't realised just how hungry she was and the bread tasted far better than it looked. She drank some water and after washing her face and hands with the ice-cold water from the jug under the window reluctantly made her way to the bed.

"Think I'll sleep with my clothes on tonight," she mused, "and tomorrow I shall see about getting as far away from here as possible and find out where the professor and the team have gone."

She lay awake on the straw mattress for a long time mulling over the events of the day. Did she really see a man murdered by these nuns or was it just her imagination? Or was it a product of the vapoury incense veil that seemed to pervade the building and had put fanciful ideas into her head?

Elaine didn't know when she drifted off to sleep but she awoke at the crack of dawn as the first rays of the sun streamed through the high barred window above her. She shuddered, partly due to the early morning cold and partly due to her recollection of the events of the previous evening, and realised that she needed the toilet. She looked at the uninviting wooden bucket and the heap of straw, "Just as well I packed a toilet roll. Previous digs and treks in remote countries have made me realise the value of something we all take for granted.

I never leave home without one in my backpack," and she gingerly approached the bucket.

* * *

A little later there was the sound of a key turning in the lock. Elaine looked up and a middle-aged nun stepped into the cell.

"I'm Sister Ingaborg and the Abbess has asked me to invite you to take breakfast with us. Every morning after Prime, the first prayers of the day, we meet in the great hall to share the first meal of the day and the Abbess believes this will be a good time for you to meet the other Sisters and become better acquainted with our Order. Please follow me," and she turned and left the cell without waiting for any response from Elaine, who hurriedly stood up and ran down the corridor so as not to lag too far behind.

Sister Ingaborg led the way along the corridor and then up several flights of stone steps into a very spacious and well-lit hall that had a large roughly hewn wooden table at its centre. Seated around this table must have been between twenty and thirty nuns who all stared intently at the newcomer as she entered the hall.

Abbess Hilda, sitting at the head of the table, beckoned Elaine to come forward and motioned towards a place at the table opposite her own, "Let me introduce you to my fellow nuns or, as I prefer to call them, my Angels. On my left is Sister Astrid, then Sister Freyja, then Sister Tusse and next to her ...."

But Elaine wasn't listening to the roll call. She was thinking to herself, "What is this all about? Who are these people and where is the team? I don't understand what's going on here at all," but she was brought back to earth as Abbess Hilda concluded, "and last of all is Sister Nissa who is the eldest of our small community. But that's enough from me for now. Join us by partaking in our humble fare."

Elaine sat down and looked at the plate set before her, "More of that black bread and a bowl of very weak-looking soup. Not much chance of getting fat while I'm here then," she mused as she picked up a wooden spoon.

"Please!" exclaimed Abbess Hilda as Elaine dipped the spoon into the soup, "Don't forget grace," and all the nuns closed their eyes and listened intently as the Abbess said a few words.

Elaine had no idea what the soup or broth was but the bread was good and filled her up. Her view was that no matter what the day ahead had in store for her she would at least not go hungry.

"Today," announced the Abbess, "we have to go over to the monastery as there are urgent matters I need to discuss with Abbott Mikell. Elaine, you will come with us," and without uttering a further word the Abbess got up and left the hall.

"We will leave shortly," added Sister Maleya, "so we'll meet you by the main door."

About half an hour later, Abbess Hilda, Sister Freyja, Sister Maleya and Elaine left the convent and walked through the extensive gardens and left by a small side gate. Elaine marvelled at the nuns working in the garden and the range of vegetables and fruit that was being cultivated. In her mind she believed that once she got to the monastery she would meet the professor and the rest of the team and find out what was really going on here.

Soon after leaving the convent grounds, and taking the path that led up to the monastery, the nuns met a group of monks coming towards them who were clearly in some sort of distress.

"Good day my brothers," the Abbess greeted them, "Pray, what brings you to the convent?"

"It's Brother Ari," replied one of the monks, "he's been missing for two days now. We've scoured the island looking for him but he's nowhere to be found and we're very worried about him. We were just coming to see if you or any of your nuns had seen him or perhaps were caring for him if he's become unwell."

"No!" retorted the Abbess immediately, "We have no truck with men, even those in holy orders."

Elaine immediately thought of the poor devil she had seen being sacrificed on the altar, "Was it real or was I just imagining it?" she thought to herself, and couldn't resist asking the question, "Can you describe Brother Ari?"

But, before any of the monks could offer a description, Abbess Hilda repeated that they hadn't seen any monks for days and said that they must press on and get to the monastery. She hadn't time to waste in idle chit-chat.

When they reached the outskirts of the monastery Elaine was surprised to see many monks at work in the extensive and well stocked gardens but, apart from a few sidelong glances, they did not pay her and the nuns any attention at all.

Once inside the building Elaine looked around and was surprised to see that it was the mirror image of the convent; same design but everything was the other way around. The tapestries and wall hangings were different of course, but the great hall, the high windows and even the rough wooden furniture, were identical. The Abbess left Elaine and the nuns to seek out the Abbott and, when the nuns wandered off, Elaine found herself on her own marvelling at the authenticity of this ancient building, "I don't understand how they can class this marvellous structure as a ruin. It looks well maintained and very much lived in. I can't wait to hear what the professor has to say about all this," and she continued to look up and admire the medieval craftsmen who had made such a magnificent building possible.

Suddenly, as she meandered through a colonnaded hall, a hand shot out and covered her mouth and another reached out and roughly pulled her behind a large column. She struggled but couldn't free herself from the vice-like grip.

"Please stop struggling to get away. Calm down and I'll take my hand away from your mouth. Nod if you promise not to scream or shout."

Elaine nodded and the hand fell from her mouth.

"What the hell are you doing?" she said in hushed but forceful tones and immediately spun round to see who had so unceremoniously dragged her behind the pillar.

"Sorry," said a rather timid looking monk, "but I had to speak to you without the others knowing."

"The others?" a startled Elaine replied, "I don't understand."

"The nuns! The nuns who brought you here! You've got to get away from them and that convent. I saw them pounce upon Brother Ari the day before yesterday and drag him into the convent. But when I spoke to the Abbott, and told him what I'd seen, he didn't believe me and refused to take the matter up with the Abbess. It's not the first time that they've kidnapped people, it's not only monks but sometimes it's strangers like you, and they're never seen again. That's why you've got to get away from that convent and leave the island. If not I dread to think what will happen to you."

Elaine began to be more than a little scared at this revelation, "But what can I do? The boat only comes to the island once a week."

"Once a week!" exclaimed the monk, "You mean once a month. Donald never comes any more frequently than that and, if the weather's bad, we can go without seeing anyone for months on end."

"What do you suggest? How can I get away?"

"Meet me tonight. When the nuns have retired to their beds for the night meet me at the back of the convent. Use the side entrance that you took to come here. I'll be waiting for you with a couple of other monks who also have their doubts about those nuns. We'll do our best to hide you until Donald next pays us a visit. Here, take this," and the monk quickly thrust a bracelet onto Elaine's right wrist.

"What's this for?" Elaine asked examining a most unusual looking bracelet which appeared to be made of solid gold and was in the form of two intertwined serpents each biting into the neck of the other.

"Take it. It's a good luck bracelet. It should give you some protection against the nuns."

"But .."

"No buts. I'll meet you tonight. But please be careful. If you're discovered then there's no telling what they'll do to you."

"I don't even know your name."

"It's Brother Edwin. Now go before they get suspicious."

Elaine turned and walked into the great hall. She was immediately confronted by the two nuns who wanted to know where she had been. When she replied that she had simply been looking round and had become engrossed in some of the stories depicted on the tapestries, and had lost track of time, they appeared to be satisfied with her explanation. All three of them returned to the main entrance and were soon met by the Abbess and the Abbott who were deep in conversation. Soon afterwards the party of nuns made its way back to the convent and, in a way, Elaine felt relieved to be back even though the words of Brother Edwin were still echoing through her mind.

* * *

The rest of the day seemed like an eternity to Elaine. In the afternoon she had helped the nuns in the garden and, even though they didn't want to engage in any meaningful conversation, she got the impression that they firmly believed they were in a bygone and tranquil age. After a dinner consisting of chunks of black bread and a really awful meat stew, Elaine retired to her cell. She was relieved that this time the nuns didn't lock it once she was inside as she had made up her mind to take up Brother Edwin's offer and leave that very night. She hastily packed her belongings and began the long wait until it was time to meet the monks.

She listened as the convent bell peeled briefly to call the nuns to Complin and eagerly awaited their return from the final prayers of the day. Once she was satisfied that the nuns had all retired and were safely asleep in their cells she gathered her belongings together and gingerly left her cell. The corridor was almost in total blackness and illuminated by just a few large candles placed in strategic places. Elaine edged her way to the end of the passageway, made her way up to the great hall, which in this half-light looked like the set from a Dracula movie, through the kitchens and out of the small side door. She looked around her and in the light of the almost full-moon could just make out three shadows standing under a small tree, "Brother Edwin?" she whispered.

"Over here," came the hushed reply, and Elaine quickly crossed the open space and made her way towards the tree. But, as she neared the monks, she was suddenly grabbed from behind and thrown violently to the ground. At the same time about a dozen nuns rushed out of the convent brandishing their long knives and attacked the unarmed monks. The fight was brief but bloody and decisive; two of the monks were killed instantly and just one managed to get away but he was wounded and left a trail of blood behind him.

"Take her to the Abbess!" one of the nuns shouted in a very authoritative manner, "She'll know what to do with her," and the nuns dragged a struggling and screaming Elaine back into the convent. Despite putting up some good resistance and trying to make use of her martial arts training Elaine was easily overpowered by the superior numbers of her attackers.

Elaine was dragged still kicking and shouting into the great hall where Abbess Hilda was sitting in a high-back chair with all the nuns arrayed neatly before her.

"Take her down to the cellar. We will then decide what to do with this traitor," she barked and the nuns once again grabbed Elaine and almost threw her down the steep stone steps that led down to the cellars. Once there she was securely tied spread-eagled on the altar.

"I had high hopes of you," the Abbess screamed at Elaine, "I even thought that you could, given time, become a member of our order. I never thought you would collude with those blasphemous monks; those monks who follow a fallen religion and call themselves holy, those monks who worship a man. Now you must pay the price, the ultimate price, with your life. Sisters, prepare for what must be done," and all the nuns fell to the ground. When they stood up again they had shed their nuns' habits and were wearing the long diaphanous near-transparent robes that Elaine recognised from her first day in the convent when she had seen the monk ceremoniously murdered.

"This is it then," Elaine thought to herself in a state of near panic as she struggled with her bonds, "now I know what happened to the professor and the team; they were all killed by these murderous nuns." And her thoughts immediately flashed back to the gypsy woman she had encountered on Liverpool Street Station who had instantly recoiled at her presence and given her the warning, "Now I know what she meant, I'm looking at a circle of nuns or rather a circle of angels, a circle of angels deep in war!"

"Make your peace with God," boomed out the Abbess almost hysterically, "as you will soon be meeting her. Then we're going to teach those monks in that monastery a lesson. They will learn that it was a mistake for the so-called orthodox and catholic churches to suppress and murder the adherents of our order all those centuries ago. Now we will take revenge and establish the true Christian religion on this island. This is just the beginning," and with one sweep of her long knife Abbess Hilda carefully but swiftly slit Elaine's clothes from the neck downwards. There was not, however, a single cut or scratch on her prostrated body.

The nuns once again fell to the floor and, when they rose again, were completely naked. They began to chant softly and then louder and louder as they walked faster and faster round and round the altar brandishing their long knives. On the command of Abbess Hilda, who was now screaming obscenities at Elaine and working the nuns into an unbridled frenzy, they stopped and raised their knives, paused for a moment, then as one plunged them deep into Elaine's prone body.

Elaine screamed.

* * *

Elaine screamed, and screamed again, and writhed in agony shouting at the top of her voice. Then she heard someone running towards her and slowly opened her eyes. To her surprise she was lying on the small track leading up the hill overlooking the convent and the monastery and Donald McDonald was running towards her puffing and panting from the exertion.

"What's the matter?" he exclaimed trying to catch his breath, "Did you fall over? Are you hurt?"

"I don't understand," Elaine blurted out almost incoherently, "the nuns, the monks," and pausing for breath added, "And you Donald. You've come back to the island."

"Come back," queried Donald with a very puzzled look on his face, "I've never left it. I had just got down the steps onto the jetty, and was about to cast off when I heard you scream, so I came straight back up here to find out what had happened. I'm not used to all this exercise at my age you know."

"But you can't have just got to the jetty. Nearly a week's gone by and those nuns; they've murdered the monks and are going to do the same to the Abbott and all those in the monastery."

"I think you've been reading too much about the history of this place. You've taken a tumble and had a bad dream."

"But it was so real. It must have happened."

"Well, I didn't want to tell you this, but I'm sure you'll hear it from your professor when you join the dig, but this year marks the five-hundredth anniversary of the abandoning of the convent and the monastery. It was five hundred years ago that the nuns of St. Gilda's, for some unknown reason, rose up from their convent and descended on the monastery of St. Gregory. All the monks were most brutally tortured and then massacred. Tradition has it that there was only one survivor, generally believed to be a certain Brother Edwin, and that he eventually managed to make his way to the king in Edinburgh. The king was outraged and sent a detachment of soldiers to the island and they showed no mercy to the nuns and they were all put to death. All, that is, except for the Abbess. She was brought back to the capital in chains and after an ecclesiastical trial was publicly hung, drawn and quartered, and her head put on a pike over the main entrance to the city. If this massacre by the nuns had taken place a few years earlier, when these islands still owed allegiance to the Danish crown, then a more terrible fate would have befallen those nuns; they would have been put to death in a most brutal fashion. Since that fateful day both the convent and the monastery have remained empty."

"A gruesome tale indeed," acknowledged Elaine, deep in thought.

"Come on," proposed Donald, "I'll give you a hand to get your stuff to the top of the hill but I can't go with you to the convent as I can't afford to miss the tide. I wouldn't want to be stranded here for the night!"

Donald carried Elaine's rucksack to the top of the hill, "There," he said, clearly out of breath, "the mist will lift shortly and you'll be able to see the convent and the monastery. I've really got to be going now. Hope you enjoy your stay and no doubt I'll see you again when I pick you up in a few weeks' time," and without further word he turned and quickly made his way down the hill towards the cliff edge and the steps leading to the jetty.

Elaine sat on her rucksack and stared down into the valley. Just as Donald had predicted the mist soon began to lift and the outlines of the two buildings came into view.

"That's odd," Elaine mused as she peered through the slowly clearing mist, "they look to be almost totally ruined, no roofs, crumbling walls, covered in moss and creepers. Surely that can't be right, they were in such good repair." But then she saw the team's tents pitched in the convent grounds and decided to make her way down into the valley so she could have a closer look and speak to the professor.

Elaine bent down to pick up her rucksack and, as she did so, she felt something fall from the inside of her sleeve and onto her right wrist. She looked down and was shocked to see it was a bracelet; a bracelet made of solid gold in the form of two intertwined serpents each biting into the neck of the other. It was the bracelet given to her by Brother Edwin.

Elaine shuddered from head to foot as a sudden realisation flashed through her whole body.

The End

*With acknowledgement to Skunk Anansie
and her song 'Weak'
from which the title of this story was taken.*

The Diabetes
Conundrum

The Diabetes Conundrum

Toby Trelawney woke up with a start and looked over at the clock. It was 7:30 in the morning but there was no sound from his wife who was sleeping beside him. She usually slept deeply and breathed heavily with the occasional snore. He raised himself up on one elbow and looked round. His wife was lying on her back staring up at the ceiling with her eyes wide open. There was no sound. He touched her arm and immediately recoiled. He recognised at once that cold clammy feeling. His wife, who suffered from type-two diabetes, was having a hypo.

Toby Trelawney swung out of bed and retrieved a small tube of glucose gel from the bedside cabinet. All he had to do was twist off the cap, squeeze the gel into his wife's mouth, massage it into his wife's gums and in fifteen or twenty minutes she would emerge from the hypo. His fingers tightened round the cap but he did not open it. Instead, his thoughts turned to events of a couple of weeks previously.

* * * * * *

He had woken early soon after five in the morning and, as he usually did on such occasions, switched on the radio to listen to the news programme on the BBC World Service. He was annoyed as his wife was snoring and breathing heavily and he had difficulty in hearing the radio clearly. However, he was still tired and soon after six he fell asleep and woke up about an hour later. He caught up with the news on Radio 4 and then realised that, apart from the radio, the room was in silence. He looked over at his wife and immediately reacted. She was lying on her back with her eyes wide open. He leant over her and moved his hand in a circular motion but her eyes did not respond. His wife was experiencing a hypo.

This was not an uncommon occurrence so Toby Trelawney immediately ran downstairs and fetched his wife's blood-sugar-level testing kit. He pricked her finger and put a small globule of blood on the test strip. He was astonished to find that the reading was only 1.6, which was very low. In the past when his wife had suffered a hypo the reading had been between 2 and 3. He searched for the glucose gel but couldn't find any tubes just some glucose tablets. He decided it would be too risky to put these in his wife's mouth as they might choke her before they dissolved. Instead he dialled 999 for an ambulance.

The ambulance arrived within ten minutes and the two-man crew immediately recognised the symptoms and confirmed the hypo. They took a blood sugar reading, which agreed with that taken earlier by Toby Trelawney, and then proceeded to insert a tube into his wife's arm through which they injected a concentrated glucose solution.

"So," enquired the elder of the ambulance men, "this isn't the first time your wife has experienced a hypo?"

"No," confirmed Toby Trelawney, "I can usually bring her round with some glucose gel but I couldn't find any this time and I felt it too risky to give her these glucose tablets. In view of the very low reading I thought it best to telephone for an ambulance." He pointed to the tablets on the bedside table.

"You did the correct thing calling us out. Now we just need a few details about your wife for our records, such as her name, date of birth, how long she's been a diabetic, her doctor's name and surgery, the medication she's currently taking, etc. By the time we've finished she should be coming out of the hypo."

"My wife's name is Sandie, that's short for Alexandra. She's now 63 and has suffered from type-two diabetes since she was about 40. She also suffers from high blood pressure and raised cholesterol. I've got a copy of her latest prescription here. It'll be easy for you to note down the medication from that," and Toby Trelawney handed the prescription to one of the ambulance men.

"My word!" said the younger of the ambulance men, "She's certainly on a lot of medication."

"What would have happened to Sandie if I hadn't woken up or had gone to work early? Would she have come round?" enquired a concerned Toby Trelawney.

"I'm afraid not," replied the elder of the two ambulance men, "she would have just drifted off."

"Drifted off? Do you mean she would have died?"

"Afraid so, she would have just slipped away. And it's more common than you would think. People often die from diabetes and its complications."

"I had no idea," replied a very worried looking Toby Trelawney.

During this rather grim exchange the paperwork was soon completed and the three men engaged in more general conversation when Toby Trelawney let it slip that he and Sandie had been married for nearly 40 years.

"Have you thought about a celebration to mark the occasion? After all, forty years together nowadays is quite an achievement. Not many marriages survive for that length of time you know."

"No, we haven't at the moment," replied Toby Trelawney, "but I have a feeling Sandie will come up with something entirely appropriate. She's very good at organising things. I usually do what she wants. I'll wait to be suitably surprised."

The two ambulance men agreed that would be the best thing to do.

"I couldn't help but notice," the younger of the two ambulance men said rather hesitantly, "that you've got a lot of Star Wars memorabilia on the landing. Have you been a fan long?"

"Ever since I saw the first film at the cinema," replied Toby Trelawney, "and I'm very proud of the collection I've managed to put together over the years. I've got most of the rare early figures but there's still a few I'm looking for. Unfortunately, the ones I'm searching for rarely appear on internet auction sites and when they do they're incredibly expensive, but I'm optimistic I'll find them all one day."

A debate then ensued between the three men about the relative merits of Star Wars, Star Trek and Doctor Who. They concluded that Star Wars and Star Trek were technically much better than early Doctor Who but that the new series of Doctor Who that had recently returned to television screens in 2005 was just as good if not better. And, of course, it was British!

Soon afterwards Sandie began to show signs of emerging from the hypo so the ambulance men took another blood sugar reading. This time it was 4.6; still low but an improvement on the previous reading. They recommended a sugary cup of tea and two slices of toast and jam.

"You must see your doctor about this and review the levels of insulin you are currently taking. Promise me you'll make an appointment today," insisted the elder of the ambulance men.

"Don't worry," Toby Trelawney immediately replied, "I'll make the appointment for her and we will see the doctor together." The ambulance crew were happy with this positive response. They packed up their equipment and returned to their vehicle.

And Toby Trelawney did what he promised the ambulance crew. He and Sandie saw a doctor later that very morning. Toby Trelawney didn't think the doctor was that much help as all she recommended was that Sandie reduce her insulin levels a little before she went to bed and monitor her blood glucose levels four times a day instead of the current two times. She did, however, prescribe some more tubes of glucose gel in case Sandie should have another hypo.

* * * * * *

Toby Trelawney then thought back further in time to his school days and his first real girlfriend; 'the Scottish girl'. He never referred to her by name because, as with 'the Scottish Play', whenever he did so it seemed to bring him bad luck. He went out with 'the Scottish girl' for two years but they had an argument on the last day at school and he never spoke to her again or bothered to find out anything about what she did after leaving school.

It was after he had been working for a year that he was reminded of 'the Scottish girl' when, quite by chance, he first saw Sandie working in an adjoining office. Although she was blonde and 'the Scottish girl' had brunette hair he couldn't help but notice that both facially and in stature they were remarkably similar. Over the next few months he and Sandie began to go out occasionally and then on a regular basis. Initially Toby Trelawney didn't think the marriage would work as she was the boss's daughter, but over the course of time it didn't seem to worry him or Sandie but it was clear that at first neither sets of parents were very keen on the match. Toby Trelawney's parents were traditional working class and both had to go out to work to support Toby and his three sisters and thought that Toby would never be accepted into an almost aristocratic family. Similarly, Sandie's parents, who were very well off and owned a number of businesses and houses, thought that Toby was out just to better himself and he didn't really care for their daughter. However, both sets of parents eventually relented and gave their blessing, and Toby and Sandie were married.

All was well for the first year of the marriage and they soon settled into a routine. Toby Trelawney left early in the morning for the long commute on the train to London and Sandie worked locally. Their lives were governed by a combination of the clock and the train timetable.

They had purchased a new-build house on the first phase of a development and so there was quite a lot of construction and building work taking place. They had become friendly with some of the supervisory staff and been able to purchase extra kitchen cabinets and other items at knock-down prices so long as 'no questions' were asked.

On the day in question, Toby Trelawney had been to a meeting away from his office and had taken the opportunity to go straight home so he could spend more time with Sandie. However, when he arrived home he found a car parked outside his house and the front door locked. He tried his key but it wouldn't fit in the lock.

This indicated that Sandie was at home with the door locked and the key still in the lock on the inside, so he rang the bell. After several bursts on the bell the door eventually opened and, much to his surprise, the works foreman rushed past him saying, "Your wife's in there," and hurriedly jumped into the car parked in front of the house and roared away.

As he entered the hall Toby Trelawney was astonished to see his wife coming down the stairs wearing just a dressing gown. She looked flustered and ill at ease.

"I'm glad you're back," she said hesitantly, "I was walking home and felt unwell by the traffic lights in town and, quite by chance, the works foreman was driving past so he gave me a lift home."

Toby Trelawney very well remembered the argument that ensued and his wife's insistence that nothing had happened or was going on with the works foreman even though he had discovered her in a state of virtual undress.

Eventually the couple patched up their differences and things settled down into a routine once more. But history was soon destined to repeat itself.

A couple of years' later Toby Trelawney once again unexpectedly came home early. This time the front door was unlocked and, as he let himself in, Toby Trelawney could hear voices in the bedroom. As he quickly made his way up the stairs he was aware of frantic movement taking place and was astonished to see his wife in bed and a man, who it transpired was an office colleague of hers who Toby had met at a recent office party, getting dressed as fast as he could.

Once again Sandie came out with the same excuse as before; she had felt unwell by the traffic lights in town on her way home and her work colleague, Michael Church, had been good enough to give her a lift home.

Toby Trelawney vividly recalled the scene with the three of them arguing and this time he firmly believed that his marriage was over. However, over the course of the next few weeks Sandie gave an undertaking that the affair was over and the couple managed to reach an understanding despite Sandie taking an overdose of Paracetamol on one occasion and Toby Trelawney having to call out the doctor. He did gain some satisfaction, however, by telephoning Michael Church's wife and acquainting her with her husband's affair. He also contacted Michael Church's management and alerted them to the situation thus ensuring that, in the light of Michael Church's field of work with vulnerable people, he would never ever gain promotion within that organisation. Toby Trelawney's view was that if he was to suffer then so should those that caused him that suffering.

A couple of years later the couple moved closer to London. Soon afterwards Sandie gave birth to twin boys and their domestic situation changed when she gave up work to look after them full-time. Toby Trelawney now had an easier journey to the office and more time to spend with his wife and family at home in the evenings. It was only when the boys were in their teens that Sandie once again went back to work.

Once the boys had married and left home Toby Trelawney's thoughts turned to early retirement but his wife seemed reluctant to give up work. Then, once again, things took a turn for the worse.

For some weeks Sandie had been seeing a female work colleague on Saturday afternoons to help her sort out her late husband's affairs after his sudden unexpected death. Toby Trelawney admired his wife for giving up her time in this selfless way but was surprised one Saturday afternoon when an envelope was pushed through the letterbox.

Inside the envelope, which was not addressed in any way, were a number of photographs. These photographs showed Sandie with a man Toby Trelawney recognised from her office, Nathan Harris. The couple were shown embracing in front of several London landmarks including HMS Belfast, Trafalgar Square and Big Ben and the Houses of Parliament; holding hands at Silverstone Racetrack and, most damning of all, in what appeared to be Nathan Harris' flat engaged in compromising positions on the bed. And, to cap it all; Toby Trelawney recognised the bed linen, duvet cover, lamp shades and several other items in that room as matching those in his guest bedroom. When he checked he found that most of that pattern of bed linen and accessories stored in the airing cupboard for use as spares or replacements had disappeared.

This was a tremendous blow to Toby Trelawney and he slumped into an armchair. He realised that, once again, his wife was up to her old tricks. He was puzzled as to the identity of the person who had posted the envelope of incriminating photographs through his door. It was obviously someone well acquainted with his wife and who very well knew what was going on and apparently disapproved of that behaviour. After all, although we now lived in a so-called enlightened and permissive society, not everyone approved of or condoned adultery. Perhaps it was a work colleague who disapproved or who was jealous. But, what was he to do about it?

He did nothing at first but the next Saturday he made a note of the mileage on the car and, as expected, when his wife returned home the car had travelled nearly 30 miles instead of the four or five that would have been expected from a drive to the other side of town and back.

Unbeknown to Toby Trelawney his wife was coming under tremendous pressure from her lover to leave her husband and so she was on the horns of a dilemma. On the one hand she believed herself to be in love with Nathan Harris but on the other hand she was not sure how her actions would be received by her family, with its strong moral traditions, and most of all by her twin boys who idolised her and who would be so disappointed and shocked at her actions. So, in a way, it was a relief when Toby Trelawney confronted her about her Saturday afternoon liaisons.

Initially she denied the affair but eventually broke down in tears and admitted to it. Toby Trelawney, who did not disclose the photographs, thought this meant the end of his marriage but, for some inexplicable reason, he and Sandie decided to give it one final chance.

Over time these events tended to fade and be almost forgotten but for some reason his wife's adulterous affairs never truly left the back of Toby Trelawney's mind, they had made an indelible impression on him, and from time-to-time they would resurface whenever he had doubts about his wife's behaviour. He was reminded of a saying from one of his favourite television programmes, "*We can never shake ourselves free of what once was – for the past stands with us like our shadow.*" He also reflected upon some prophetic words he had read in a book entitled 'The Christmas Present' by the actress turned author Rène Ray, in which one of her characters states, "Everyone knew that men sowed their wild oats before they married – and women *afterwards.*" How true that had proved to be in the case of Sandie; not on one occasion but on several. She had proved to be nothing short of a serial adulteress.

Toby Trelawney could never understand why, when he had never strayed from the straight and narrow and had always been entirely faithful to his wife, that she had betrayed him in this way on so many occasions. Did she really think so little of him? Had she no regard or feelings for him at all? Had their marriage been nothing more than a sham? He had been tempted in the past, especially at his office's infamous Christmas parties, where he had been approached by some very beautiful women, but he had always resisted that temptation. He very well knew the risks and didn't want to prejudice his marriage or cause Sandie any distress even though he himself had experienced such great anguish by his wife's behaviour. He was also aware of the devastating effect such affairs coming to light would have on the twin boys and he wanted to spare them that pain.

Toby Trelawney also thought about all the good times he and Sandie had experienced together. They both shared a love of the theatre and he reflected upon the many times they had driven up to London or taken the train to the West End and the numerous premieres they had attended, even meeting some of the cast backstage afterwards for autographs.

A love of art had also resulted in them visiting many of the great art galleries of Europe and North America as well as in the United Kingdom. This travelling had given them the idea of visiting all counties within England and this they had achieved only about a year previously. Recently they had started planning trips to Scotland and Wales, two parts of the United Kingdom they had wanted to visit for a long time.

And as Toby Trelawney thought about his wife's past behaviour, both good and bad, his thoughts turned to events of only a week ago. As had become the norm they would both walk into town and, once there, Sandie would look round the shops and Toby Trelawney would go for a walk along the river and they would meet back home for a mid-morning cup of tea and a biscuit.

On that occasion they had walked into town as usual and after going in a couple of shops Toby Trelawney had left his wife and strode down the hill towards the river. However, once he got a few hundred yards along the narrow path his way was blocked by some fallen trees that had blown down in the previous night's gales so he had no alternative but to retrace his steps back to town.

It was when he walked into the town square that he received the shock of his life. There was Sandie in deep conversation with a man Toby Trelawney was certain had worked with his wife up to her retirement of a few years ago. They were standing very close together and seemed to be gazing into each other's eyes. Toby Trelawney was incandescent with rage but managed to control his feelings and made his way home by another route so that he was not seen by the pair. His wife returned home about 30 minutes later and, although mentioning a conversation with one of their neighbours, made no mention of her meeting with an old office colleague. Toby Trelawney remained silent on the matter but within he was seething and was determined to find out more.

The next day he left his wife in town as usual but instead of making his way to the river walk Toby Trelawney doubled back and, as he suspected, Sandie once again met her former office colleague. He was intrigued but decided not to mention this to his wife until he had observed them again. Unfortunately this would not be the case as the very next morning Sandie had suffered another hypo and was now lying next to Toby Trelawney unconscious.

* * * * * *

Toby Trelawney tore himself away from thoughts of the past and looked across at his wife who was lying on her back with wide open eyes staring blankly at the ceiling completely oblivious to the world around her. He had taken just a few moments to reflect on the many good points of his long marriage together with the numerous bad points. He reluctantly picked up the tube of glucose gel from the bedside cabinet and deliberately caressed it gently between his fingers. Slowly his fingers tightened and grasped the cap and came to a stop. Toby Trelawney thought briefly then twisted off the cap and emptied the contents of the tube..........*into his own mouth*! He lay back on the bed and continued listening to the radio and, as he became engrossed in world affairs once more, a glimmer of a smile slowly spread across his face.

* * * * * *

Sandie's funeral took place three weeks' later at a local crematorium. She had been a very popular person, both at work and in the community, and the chapel was crowded. Indeed, there were many people standing at the rear of the room who were unable to find seats. About half way through the ceremony, after the local Methodist minister had officiated, Toby Trelawney rose and made his way to the lectern to make his tribute. Those who followed his every word may have noticed a tremor and a slight hesitation in his voice towards the end of his speech and put this down to the emotion of the occasion and his recent bereavement. But this was not the case. As he was concluding his speech Toby Trelawney's attention was drawn to a latecomer who squeezed through the heavy chapel doors and who stood with bowed head in a corner. It was none other than the former work colleague of his late wife who he had seen in very close conversation with her in town.

"What a nerve!" he thought to himself as he made his way back to his seat, "I'll have a word with him later." But the opportunity never arose because of the sheer number of people present who all seemingly wanted to talk to him about Sandie and share their memories of her with him.

Later, at the wake in the Black Lion pub, Toby Trelawney made a point of circulating freely and chatting to those present hoping to catch sight of Sandie's former work colleague but he did not appear to be present.

"Obviously he didn't have the guts to face me," he thought, "but I'll keep an eye open for him whenever I'm in town. I'll get him one day!"

* * * * * *

One afternoon a few days later there was a knock on Toby Trelawney's front door. He put down his newspaper and opened the door. There, standing directly in front of him, was none other than the individual he had seen chatting so intently to his wife in town and who he had later seen at the back of the crematorium.

"You don't know me Mister Trelawney but many years ago I was a work colleague of your wife's. May I come in?"

"Certainly," replied Toby Trelawney and he stepped aside so the individual could pass into the sitting room, "*but you may not be leaving in one piece*!" he thought to himself as he gestured towards a rather elegant arm chair.

"My name is Frank Bell and many years ago I worked with your wife. I took early retirement and lost track of all my fellow work colleagues but, quite by chance, I met Sandie about a week before her most untimely death. Please accept my most sincere condolences, by the way."

Toby Trelawney did not reply. Instead he sat passively and stared directly at Frank Bell.

"I hope you didn't mind," Frank Bell continued, "but when I heard about Sandie's passing I just had to go to the funeral service and pay my respects but I didn't think it appropriate to attend the wake in the Black Lion as I hadn't been invited."

Toby Trelawney remained silent seething within.

"Anyway, to cut a long story short, after Sandie and I had reminisced about old times she told me that your fortieth wedding anniversary was just a few weeks away and she was looking to buy you something special. She remembered that like you I had always been a very keen Star Wars collector and had several rare figures and she wondered if I might be able to suggest somewhere she could buy one of the few figures you were still looking for. As luck would have it I had recently started to sell some of my rarer figures to raise a bit of money. You see my pension has turned out to be a lot less than I thought and selling some of the rarer figures would give me some additional income. Anyway, would you believe, I still had one of the figures she was looking for. So we agreed to meet again so I could show her the figure and we could perhaps agree on a price but, unfortunately, that meeting was destined never to take place."

Toby Trelawney remained seated still not saying a word.

"Anyway, I don't want to take up any more of your time than is necessary at this very sad time, but my reason for visiting you today is to give you this," and Frank Bell handed Toby Trelawney a package in which was one of the very rare boxed early Star Wars figures that he had been searching for, and unable to find, for so many years.

"I would like you to accept this as a reminder of your wife, of Sandie, and the nearly forty years of marriage you had together. I certainly won't take any money for it but I'd like to think that every time you look at this figure it will remind you of your wife, of Sandie, and all she meant to you!"

The End

> "In a lifetime, in every act among the seeds we sow, is the seed of tragedy; and tragedy is a plant that can take many years to grow, and even longer to blossom and bear its bitter fruit."
>
> From 'Who Pays the Ferryman?' by Michael J Bird

Firewood

Firewood

"Well, what have you managed to find? Hope it's not as bad as the last few days," shouted Stan Finbow as he rushed out of the rather ancient building that housed his failing antique furniture business and opened the tailgate of the equally antique van that sported his name on all sides.

Two weary-looking men in their early sixties almost fell out of the cab and ran round to the back, "Don't get too excited, there's not much here," said John Carberry the taller of the two."

"That's right," chipped in his partner Geoff Kemp, "there's just not much about nowadays in this town. And if there is, everybody watches the antiques programmes on the telly and thinks they're sitting on a fortune. They think they're all experts and just won't sell for a reasonable price anymore."

"Let's have a look and see what you've brought me," and Stan helped the two men to carry the items of furniture into the warehouse.

"To say I'm disappointed would be an understatement," exclaimed Stan as he examined the rather tatty and battered collection of furniture that had all seen better days, "This stuff is rubbish, even by your recent standards. Look at it! How am I going to sell it? I hope you didn't spend too much of my hard-earned money on it. This business is going down the pan fast and it's you two who are to blame! Soon we'll all be on the dole."

"We do our best," pleaded John, "but there's just nothing out there. It's like Geoff said, when we find something half decent nobody wants to sell for the prices we're prepared to pay."

"Drastic action! Drastic action! That's what's needed," exclaimed Stan as an idea came to him, "Look, why don't you try that new estate on the southern edge of town. There's bound to be something down there."

"I don't know," said a worried-looking Geoff, "whenever we've tried the newer areas in the past there's never been anything worth-while."

"Be that as it may, you get down there tomorrow and don't bother coming back here unless you've got a van load of decent furniture. Understood?"

"Crystal clear," replied John and Geoff in unison and they returned wearily to the van.

* * *

The next day the two of them went round the new estate as suggested by Stan but the exercise yielded precious little. It wasn't so much that people weren't willing to sell but more that they had nothing to sell. Still, the pair did manage to purchase a few nice items, mainly of low value, and they hoped that would be sufficient to ward off Stan's wrath.

"Is this it?" screeched Stan when he saw the fruits of the pair's labour, "This is all you managed to get. Call yourselves professionals! This is appalling! I'm going to give you one last chance. Otherwise, you're both fired. Is that understood?" said Stan using his often repeated catchphrase.

"I've an idea," John announced suddenly, "why don't we try some of the outlying villages? We could concentrate on the older cottages, possibly those a bit off the beaten track, where we might find older people with some nice pieces to sell."

"That's a good idea," agreed Stan, "I can't believe I didn't think of it before. Here, take this," and he handed a large wad of notes to John, "Don't disappoint me."

* * *

John and Geoff spent the morning knocking on doors in the first village they came across but, apart from a few small items of furniture, didn't have much success. Usually they were greeted with hostility and told to 'clear off' in no uncertain manner.

"I don't understand these people," said a down-hearted Geoff, "we've put on our best clothes and still they don't trust us. Must be that clapped-out van of Stan's, he should invest in a new one."

"I've an idea," piped-up John, "why don't we...."

"Another idea," interrupted Geoff, "I thought this idea was yours!"

"I know, I know," John began to explain, "Let's go to a much smaller village. I know one close to where I grew up and it's not far from here. It's quite tiny but a lot of the older people have lived there for years and they're bound to have some nice things. It'll be up to us to persuade them to part company with them. Come on we can get there in less than an hour."

Nearly an hour later the battered old van arrived at the end of a small lane sporting an unmade gravel road and Geoff and John began to knock on doors. John was correct in assuming that the lane would be occupied predominantly by elderly people, but none of them were interested in selling furniture or other antiques that had been in their families often for many years.

"Here we are," said a resigned John, "the last cottage in the lane. Let's both go to this one and see what we can find," and the two of them walked up the narrow uneven shrub-lined path and lifted the heavy metal knocker. Before the sound of the knocker was heard striking the solid oak door it opened as if by itself.

Both men stepped back in amazement. A rather shabbily dressed frail-looking man who must have been in his late eighties opened the door.

"We could be onto a winner here," whispered Geoff, "Let's try and get inside and see what he's got."

"Good morning, sir," said John putting on a false posh accent, "We represent Finbow Antiques and we're in the area paying the best prices for furniture and other antique items. Hopefully, we can take away any old items you no longer require and transform them into ready cash for you. Here!" and John took the bundle of notes from his pocket and deliberately showed them to the old man.

"I don't know," said the old man in a faltering voice, "I've been warned not to let strangers into my cottage. You never know who to trust nowadays. Things aren't like they were in my day you know."

"You've nothing to fear from us," responded Geoff quickly, "we're almost the same generation as you, we know how you feel and we couldn't agree more. That's why we've come in a van that shows who we work for and, just to show you that everything's above board, we give receipts for everything we buy. What could be fairer than that?"

The old man briefly hesitated while he thought about what Geoff had said then looked him straight in the eye and invited the two men inside.

"My name's John and this is my partner Geoff, and we work for Stan Finbow the owner of the business," said John reassuringly as he bent his head down to go through the rather low door, and entered the cottage which must have been all of three or four hundred years old.

"My name's Bill, Bill Hailstone," said the elderly man, but John and Geoff hardly paid him any attention as they looked around this veritable Aladdin's cave filled with antique furniture.

"We're onto a winner here if we can get him to sell any of this stuff. Just look at the quality," whispered John, "We'll try the old trick of building up his confidence. We'll offer him over the odds for a few pieces then once he thinks we're on the level we'll make a killing by getting anything decent at a much lower price by saying it's not worth as much as he thought it was."

"What's that you're saying? My hearing's not all it used to be," said Bill struggling to listen to the two men's conversation.

"We were just saying how nice and cosy it is in here," said Geoff reassuringly, "and that we could be interested in buying a few bits and pieces. If you want to sell that is," he quickly added. "Why don't you make us a cup of tea and we'll have a look around to see if there's anything we're interested in."

"I'll do that," agreed Bill, and he slowly made his way to the adjoining kitchen from where he could still keep an eye on the two men.

"This place is a gold mine. Look at those chairs, that table, must be at least three hundred years old and in

immaculate condition. I think we're going to do all
….." but John's words were cut short as he spotted a
large cabinet in the corner of the room.

"See that!" exclaimed John under his breath, "That's
a Louis Quinze, must be worth at least twenty-five
thousand pounds, that's what we've got to set our sights
on getting."

"Couldn't agree more," said Geoff as he went into
the kitchen to give Bill a hand with the tea.

"Very kind of you I'm sure," said Bill as he sat down
and the three of them drank their tea.

"Have you lived here long, Bill?"

"All of my life. There's been Hailstones in this village
since the Fourteenth Century. You can check the Parish
records if you don't believe me."

"We believe you Bill. Tell me, have you got any
family in the village?"

"No, my wife's been dead for nearly twenty five years
and my two children have both moved away to the
town. I seldom see them nowadays, but I've got some
good neighbours who keep an eye on me and see that I
don't come to any harm."

"That's nice," acknowledged Geoff, "it's good to
have neighbours who care."

"You've certainly got a nice cottage here and some lovely old furniture. Would you consider selling any of it?" enquired John.

"Well, I could do with a bit of extra money. I've had a few unexpected expenses lately and the pension as you know doesn't go very far nowadays."

"Quite so," said an understanding Geoff, "If we can help in any way then we'd be more than pleased to do so."

"That's very kind of you," and Bill pointed to a few items of furniture that he would be prepared to part with.

John estimated that in normal circumstances he would have paid close to three hundred pounds but offered Bill four hundred and fifty pounds.

"Are you sure?" asked a surprised Bill, "I've had other antique dealers make me offers but they've only been about half of what you're prepared to pay."

"As I said before, we're not here to rip you off. We're here to give you a fair price for anything we buy," said a very sincere-sounding Geoff and he and John loaded the items into the van.

The two men came back into the cottage and deliberately counted out the notes one at a time into Bill's hands so he could appreciate just how much money he was getting. Then, just as they were leaving and almost as an after-thought, Geoff said, "That cabinet in the corner looks interesting, would you be prepared to sell it?"

"No, I don't think so. It has a certain sentimental attachment. I couldn't sell it."

"Well, we'll be in the area again next week so perhaps we'll call in for another chat. Who knows, if we make you a good offer you might be prepared to let it go."

"I don't think so, but please pop in by all means. It's nice to have a bit of company for a change and you two look like people I can trust."

"Take care!" exclaimed John and he and Geoff returned to the van for the journey back to the antiques warehouse.

"I think Stan's going to be very pleased with us this time," said John as he drove the van slowly out of the village towards the town.

* * *

"You paid how much for this stuff?" ranted Stan as he looked at the items John and Geoff placed before him, "I'll be lucky to get two or three hundred pounds for the lot of it and you paid four hundred and fifty! I don't believe it. You've finally flipped and gone mad!"

"Hear us out, please. We're onto a winner here," and John explained about the veritable treasure trove in Bill's cottage.

"It better be as good as you say it is. Tell me, what's this cabinet like?"

"It's definitely French and a Louis Quinze. Must be worth twenty five thousand, might even fetch close to thirty thousand."

"Are you sure?"

"Completely, that's why we paid over the odds for this lot. Bill thinks we pay fair prices so when we say the cabinet is a reproduction, but a good one at that, he'll believe what we say, a couple of grand at most."

"I hope you're right. I can't afford any slip-ups. If this deal falls through then the business will be ruined. When are you seeing him again?"

"Middle of next week."

"Then don't disappoint me. In the meantime you can concentrate your efforts on other villages. Who knows you might have similar luck. Perhaps our fortunes have at last changed for the better."

* * *

"Here we are again," said John as he turned the van into the narrow lane and parked in front of Bill Hailstone's small cottage.

The two men walked up the narrow garden path and the door opened just before they reached it.

"Come on in," said an enthusiastic Bill who beckoned them inside, "I've put the kettle on and the tea will be ready shortly. Hope you find some more items of interest that you want to buy."

"I'm sure we will," agreed a smiling Geoff as he cast an eye around the room.

"You've got some more furniture in the room," said a surprised John after spotting some very nice antique pieces that weren't there the previous week.

"I thought you might be interested in them so I brought them in from the shed."

"The shed!" exclaimed John, "You kept furniture of this quality in the shed!"

"Best place for it. I had no use for it all so why clutter up the inside of the cottage? It's small enough as it is. Is this stuff of any use? Do you want to take it off my hands?"

"We'll certainly take these pieces off your hands," said John and, as he did the last time, he offered Bill a sum of money way over what the items were really worth. This was readily agreed to by Bill who couldn't believe his luck to have met two such honest and reasonable dealers.

"Before we go," said John, "we wondered if you'd had any further thoughts about selling that cabinet," and he pointed towards the Louis Quinze cabinet.

"No, I couldn't sell it," replied Bill, "it means too much to me."

"Pity," said John, "we could make you a good offer," but going closer he added, "Oh no, I think it's a reproduction. What do you think, Geoff?"

Geoff went over to the cabinet and pretended to examine it closely.

"I'm afraid John's right. How could we have been fooled by it? Having said that, it's a very good reproduction, possibly turn of the last century. I suppose we could still be interested," he said hesitantly, "but we couldn't offer anything close to what an original one would be worth."

"My father said that cabinet has been in the family for years and years and I shouldn't ever sell it. He said it was my inheritance and I should hang onto it come what may."

"That's all well and good but if you want to sell we could give you five hundred pounds for it. Even at that price we'd be pushed to make a profit on it but we're willing to take a chance."

"No," replied Bill emphatically, "I couldn't sell it."

"Well no sweat, it's of no real value but there is a lot of wood in it. You could always use it as firewood," joked Geoff in an effort to get Bill to part with the cabinet, but with no success.

"Think about it," suggested John, "We'll be in the area again next week so we'll pop in and see if you've changed your mind.

"You are certainly more than welcome to come back next week but I don't think I'll be changing my mind."

* * *

"What do you mean you didn't get the cabinet!" exclaimed an almost apoplectic Stan, "And in the bargain you spent more of my hard-earned money on another load of rubbish furniture! I'm not happy at all."

"Calm down, Bill's going to reflect on our offer. We're certain he'll think about it and decide to sell. He trusts us, he knows we won't rip him off," said Geoff trying to pacify Stan.

"You two are bloody useless! I don't know why I employ you! I could do better myself!"

"Then why don't you?" challenged John, "If you think we're that bad and you could do better then you go and speak to the old boy. Let's see if you can get him to sell!"

"You're on! Next week I'll go with you. I'll show you how to get the better of a half-senile old man. Look and learn!"

* * *

A week later the battered old van made its way up to Bill Hailstone's small cottage and, as soon as it came to a halt, Bill opened the heavy oak front door.

"I thought you said he was a scruffy old sod," remarked Stan as he saw Bill standing in the doorway wearing what could only be described as a very expensive well-cut suit.

"He was the last couple of times we saw him. Perhaps he's gone and paid a visit to Oxfam!" grumbled John.

"Hello Bill," enthused Geoff, "We told our boss all about you and he thought he'd come along personally to meet you. Hope you don't mind?"

"No, not at all," replied Bill, "The more the merrier. I like to have a bit of company to brighten up my life. Come on in all of you."

"Nice place you have here Bill," said Stan, casting an eye around the room trying to find the Louis Quinze cabinet.

"Glad you like it. You make yourself at home. I'll make us all a nice cup of tea and then you can tell me what you'd like to buy this week."

As Bill made his way slowly to the kitchen Stan turned to John and Geoff and said in hushed tones, "Well, where is it then? I don't see any Louis Quinze cabinet. There's plenty of other stuff here but no sign of that cabinet."

"Don't worry, I'll ask Bill when he's made the tea," and turning towards the kitchen John called out, "Bill, old mate, I'll come and give you a hand," and he left the room.

When all four of them were sitting round a small early Victorian games table that Stan had admired as soon as he entered the room the subject eventually got round to the cabinet in question.

"I was telling Stan all about that reproduction Louis Quinze cabinet you showed us last time we were here, but that you didn't want to sell it," said John in the hope of getting Bill to change his mind.

"My old dad used to say that cabinet was my inheritance and I should look after it and never sell it," said Bill rather sadly, "so I took his advice."

Puzzled by this remark Geoff asked the question they all wanted an answer to, "Actually Bill, I can't see the cabinet. What have you done with it?"

"Oh, I've taken it into the scullery," replied Bill in a most casual manner.

"The scullery!" retorted Geoff, "You've put a piece of furniture of that age and quality in the scullery!"

"Best place for it!" retorted Bill.

"Is it all right if I take Stan through to the scullery to have a look at it?" enquired Geoff getting somewhat hot under the collar in the presence of his boss.

"Of course, through the door and you'll find it on your left."

Geoff led Stan through the door and as soon as they entered the scullery they stopped transfixed in their tracks.

"What have you done?" exclaimed Geoff falling to his knees and almost crying, "What have you done?"

"I took your advice and chopped up the cabinet for firewood," replied an apparently unconcerned Bill still drinking his tea, "Biscuit anyone?"

"His advice!" bellowed Stan who was now fast becoming distraught and visibly angry, "Are you telling me that Geoff told you to chop up a cabinet worth between twenty five and thirty thousand pounds?" he shouted, forgetting how much Geoff had actually offered to pay for it.

"What do you mean twenty five or thirty thousand pounds? He said I'd be lucky to get five hundred pounds for it and when I refused to sell it he said I might as well use it for firewood, so that's what I've done. I chopped it up to put on the fire."

"That's awful," stammered Geoff who still couldn't believe the evidence of his own eyes. "I can't remember the last time I saw a cabinet like that in such good condition. And now it's all gone. How could you take my remark so seriously?"

Stan turned to face Bill and said, "You stupid old git! Not only have you destroyed a priceless cabinet but you've lost the chance to make yourself a lot of money."

"I thought about Geoff's offer long and hard," replied Bill in subdued tones deliberately ignoring Stan's insult, "I remembered what my old dad told me about this being my inheritance. Then I decided to chop it up and see what my old dad was on about. And do you know what I found?"

"Surprise us," said Stan in a most sarcastic tone of voice, "Tell us, what did you find?"

"It came as a complete surprise but my old dad was telling the truth after all. That cabinet was indeed my inheritance. As I split the back open I discovered a small secret compartment and inside was hidden a dried-up leather pouch containing over 500 old gold coins. I had to wait until last Saturday to take them into town as the bus only runs at weekends but I took them into the local museum. They advised me to put them into a specialist auction in London at the end of the month and reckon they'll fetch nearly a million pounds."

Stan beckoned to John and Geoff and the trio left the cottage in silence and trudged wearily back to the van.

Inside the cottage Bill put some more wood on the fire and smiled as he looked up at the mantelpiece and a rather faded photograph of his father, "Cheers dad, you were right all along about my inheritance!"

The End

In search of
Lenten Thoughts

In Search of Lenten Thoughts

This short story was inspired
by the following poem

Lenten Thoughts of a High Anglican
by John Betjeman

Isn't she lovely, "the Mistress"?
With her wide-apart grey-green eyes,
The droop of her lips and, when she smiles,
Her glance of amused surprise?

How nonchalantly she wears her clothes,
How expensive they are as well!
And the sound of her voice is as soft and deep
As the Christ Church tenor bell.

But why do I call her "the Mistress"
Who know not her way of life?
Because she has more of a cared-for air
Than many a legal wife.

How elegantly she swings along
In the vapoury incense veil;
The angel choir must pause in song
When she kneels at the altar rail.

The preacher said that we should not stare
Around when we come to church,
Or the Unknown God we are seeking
May forever elude our search.

But I hope that the preacher will not think
It unorthodox and odd
If I add that I catch in "the Mistress"
A glimpse of the Unknown God.

Lenten Thoughts of a High Anglican is reproduced by kind
permission of John Murray

The events in this story take place
in 1975 and 1976

In Search of Lenten Thoughts

"Children's Favourites! Not again," said Jackie as she cleared the breakfast things from the table.

"Saturday isn't Saturday without 'Children's Favourites'. It's the best programme on Radio 4," replied her husband Geoff, "No," he corrected himself, "It's the best programme on radio anywhere. I know it's made up of requests from children but it really does cover a vast range of tastes. One of the things I like about it is you never know just what is going to be played next," and he took a last sip of his tea before an over enthusiastic Jackie snatched his cup away and casually dropped it into a sink of hot soapy water.

"Come on, you know where the tea towel is!" Jackie playfully teased her husband and plunged her hands into the foaming bowl to retrieve the breakfast crockery.

Geoff reluctantly grabbed the tea towel and began to dry up the crockery. Suddenly he threw down the tea towel and focused his attention on the radio. "I know that poem," he said as he struggled to listen to the broadcast, "But I've never heard it set to music before," and he stood motionless by the radio enthusiastically taking in every word.

"The Cockney Amorist, that's it, the Cockney Amorist," he exclaimed as the music came to an end, and he waited impatiently for 'Stewpot', the name affectionately given to the presenter Ed Stewart by his young listeners, to offer a comment.

"Now that was an unusual song, or should I say poem set to music, from the Poet Laureate Sir John Betjeman; it's from his latest LP entitled 'Betjeman's Banana Blush'. Now next is a request from ......" but Geoff had turned his attention away from the radio and had grabbed a pencil and pad to write down the details of that extraordinary listening experience.

"Betjeman's Banana Blush, eh!" he mumbled to himself and then rather reluctantly turned his attention to the pile of breakfast dishes that had mounted up on the draining board while his attention had been focussed on matters far from the sink. "Do you know, dear?" he said with a glazed look in his eyes while drying the same cup over and over, "I'd like to know a bit more about that LP."

"Well, if you take me shopping this afternoon then perhaps we'll have time to have a look in Andy's Records; I'm sure they'll stock the LP, particularly if it's a recent release."

"It's a deal," agreed Geoff and he tackled the remainder of the drying up with a renewed vigour that took Jackie completely by surprise.

After a somewhat hectic afternoon's shopping, during which Jackie had managed to convince Geoff that she needed a new dress and matching shoes for his fiftieth birthday celebrations the following month, they managed to find their way into Andy's Records with about 15 minutes remaining before closing time. Geoff eagerly scanned the shelves and LP racks but couldn't find the John Betjeman LP anywhere despite searching under a number of different categories. In desperation he sought out a member of staff.

"Excuse me. I wonder if you can help me. I'm looking for an LP called 'Betjeman's Banana Blush' but I can't find it anywhere in the racks."

The shop assistant, who pointedly looked at his watch as if to emphasise the imminent closure of the store, somewhat reluctantly retrieved a large portfolio from behind the counter. After thumbing through its pages in what appeared to be a rather haphazard way the assistant placed the heavy tome on the counter, "Here, I think this is what you're looking for," and he spun the volume round to face Geoff who avidly read the entry indicated by the assistant's outstretched finger.

"Look at this," he remarked excitedly to both Jackie and the assistant and quoted from the entry, "Betjeman's Banana Blush. Sir John Betjeman the Poet Laureate reads his verse accompanied by the music of Jim Parker." He paused, then added, "And these are the poems on the LP," and he read the list out aloud, much to the annoyance of not only the shop assistant but also his wife who, after an afternoon's shopping, really was anxious to get home and relax,

"Indoor Games Near Newbury
Business Girls
Agricultural Caress
Youth and Age on Beaulieu River, Hants
The Arrest of Oscar Wilde at The Cadogan Hotel
Lenten Thoughts
The Cockney Amorist
Longfellow's Visit to Venice
The Flight from Bootle
A Shropshire Lad
On A Portrait of A Deaf Man
A Child Ill

There are some good poems here," he mused and, after a slight pause, turned towards his wife. "This LP was released by Charisma Records in 1974, that's only last year, but I must confess I've never heard of it before. Thank goodness for 'Stewpot' and Children's Favourites!"

The shop assistant looked at his watch once more, "I'm afraid we're about to close, sir."

"That's all right. We'll take it. I'll order that LP now."

"Very good, sir, I'll just take a few details and will send the order off first thing on Monday morning. Will probably take a week to get here so I suggest you call back next Saturday."

"That's fine," he replied and, after leaving his name, address and telephone number, an excited Geoff left the shop and was followed by Jackie who now found herself carrying her own rather heavy bags as her husband, in his new-found excitement, was completely oblivious to her plight.

Relaxing after dinner Jackie tried on her new clothes. They were much more expensive than she had originally budgeted for, but both she and Geoff agreed that they were ideal for their weekend in London when they would celebrate Geoff's fiftieth birthday by staying for two luxury nights at the Savoy Hotel and going to watch Alan Ayckbourn's play 'Confusions' at the Apollo Theatre.

"Not long to go now, next week's August and two weeks after that it's your birthday. I've been thinking ……"

"Now I'm worried!" interjected Geoff.

"Seriously," sighed Jackie, "I've been thinking that perhaps I should buy you that LP. I've been trying to think of a few small things to get you in addition to your main present, and that LP would be just fine."

"It's a deal," agreed Geoff, "But make sure it's well hidden or else I won't be able to resist the temptation to play it!"

"A deal," endorsed Jackie as she and Geoff exchanged a brief kiss and she went upstairs to change into some less formal clothes.

* * *

Jackie was not by nature a cruel person but, on this occasion, she excelled herself and made Geoff wait until after their return from London on the Sunday evening before allowing him to open his small presents. Despite his anticipation, he left the LP until last, and pointedly opened the other presents first. This was not difficult because although Jackie had wrapped it up very carefully the distinctive shape of an LP made disguising it very difficult.

Geoff carefully examined the package then removed the ribbon, peeled off the Sellotape from the coloured paper and delicately extracted the LP. Here in all its glory was the prize he had waited so patiently for over the last three weeks. He held it up in front of him and admired the front cover; a picture of a smiling Sir John Betjeman. He turned the LP over and was greeted by a number of photographs of Sir John, obviously taken during the recording sessions as he was wearing headphones, together with a list of the poems featured on the LP.

"Looking at those photographs Sir John certainly had great fun recording this LP so I think I'm going to enjoy it. As you know I've got several volumes of his poems but not many recordings of him actually reading them so I'm looking forward to this," and he very carefully took the gleaming black vinyl disc from its sleeve and, holding it delicately by its edges, he held it up to reflect the light and ensure that there were no scratches before placing it on his record deck. Gently closing the smoked-plastic top he switched on the record player and sat back in his white leather armchair in great anticipation. Jackie took the opportunity to leave the room and disappear upstairs for a long soak in the bath.

Geoff eagerly awaited the first poem, 'Indoor Games Near Newbury' and was not disappointed. He was familiar with this poem from one of the many collections of Sir John's works that were regularly published by John Murray but did not recall having heard it read by Sir John himself. Oddly enough, having the musical accompaniment of Jim Parker seemed to make it all the more entertaining, and Geoff enjoyed the combination of Sir John's words and Jim Parker's distinctive musical style that had obviously been specially written for this very poem.

Slumped in his armchair Geoff was lost to the world and felt most disappointed when 'A Child Ill' came to an end and the LP finished.

"What a fantastic record!" thought Geoff as he returned to the record deck and played the LP once more, "Can't wait to hear them all again," and he resumed his rather ungainly posture in the armchair.

"I think the charm of this LP lies not only in the poems being read by Sir John himself, although I have long believed that he reads his work much better than others who often narrate his poems on the radio," Geoff pondered to himself, "But also by the eclectic mix of subjects. There are humorous poems, nostalgic poems that echo long-forgotten days of England, some sad poems and even a few historical ones for good measure;

and of course, that music which perfectly complements each poem and so expertly sets the mood for the listener." He tried to categorise 'The Cockney Amorist', the poem that he had originally heard on the radio and which had prompted him to seek out a copy of this LP and he came to the conclusion that it was a blend of nostalgia and sadness. "Altogether a very enjoyable experience." he nodded to himself.

The more Geoff thought about the LP the more he believed that this was his best fiftieth birthday present. The weekend in London had been very enjoyable but was over, it was consigned to the past, whereas the LP would be something he could treasure and play whenever he wanted.

He carefully retrieved the LP from the record deck, placed it inside its protective paper sleeve and slipped it back in the large yellow, pink and blue outer card sleeve. Looking down the list of poems printed on the back of the sleeve Geoff realised that somewhere, in his collection of Sir John's poetry, he had the words to all of the poems featured except one, 'Lenten Thoughts'; this was the only poem he had not heard before.

"Think I'll play that track again," he said to himself and walked over to the record deck, extracted the disc and very delicately indeed placed the stylus in the groove between the fifth and sixth tracks, "Wouldn't do to scratch it."

All too soon the track was finished but Geoff felt he needed to listen to it again so rather wearily he got up from his chair, stopped the turntable, and once more placed the stylus between tracks five and six. But, about three and a half minutes later, when the track once again finished he had to repeat the process, "Pity they can't think of a way so that you can select a track and make it play repeatedly until you're fed up with it."

This continued for about a further three or four times until Jackie came back to the lounge and promptly switched the record player off. "I've heard that song or poem or whatever you want to call it once too often!" she complained, "Can't you play anything else?"

"Sorry dear, I suppose I did get a bit carried away," Geoff admitted, "but this LP is really wonderful and I'm delighted with it, especially this particular track. I've never heard this poem before and I'm fascinated by it. I think Sir John's captured the spirit of the central character very well. In just a few words we build up a mental picture and learn so much about that woman. Or do we?" he reflected, "We don't get to know her name or where she lives or what she does for a living. Perhaps that's the key to the poem's charm; we're left with an enigma, a mystery that tantalises us and leaves us wanting more."

"It's just a poem, nothing more. I don't know why you're getting so worked up about it," Jackie teased, "Now let's settle down and relax, watch a bit of television, after all we've got to get up early tomorrow for work. Monday morning will soon be here."

"I suppose you're right," acknowledged Geoff, and he reluctantly took the LP and placed it in pride of place in the rack under the record deck.

* * *

Over the next couple of weeks, following the excitement of Geoff's fiftieth birthday celebrations and the weekend away in London, things soon returned to normal. Work and family matters once again dominated his life but Geoff still couldn't get 'Lenten Thoughts' out of his mind. Whenever the opportunity arose he would play the LP but more and more he would play just that single track over and over again and this began to infuriate his wife.

"I'm getting fed up with that blasted LP. All you ever do is listen to that record. What is it about that particular track? Even I know every single word of it by heart now! I'm getting concerned about you; it's becoming an obsession. I'm worried it's beginning to dominate your life," protested Jackie, but Geoff just shrugged his shoulders.

"I don't know," he admitted, "It's almost like a drug. I just can't stop listening to it. I feel that I know that woman, the 'Mistress', but do I? It's a great poem but Sir John really tells us so very little about her. Perhaps that's the secret of why it's so alluring and intriguing."

"Well, if you feel that strongly about it and want to know more, why not write to Sir John and ask him. Ask him to tell you about the woman, who she is, and why he felt the need to write about her in that way."

"What a brilliant idea!" exclaimed Geoff, "Now why didn't I think of it?"

"Well you don't honestly expect to receive a reply from him do you?"

"Of course he'll reply. I recall reading somewhere that he always attends to his correspondence personally. Admittedly, I don't know his address but I'm sure I can write to him via his publishers, John Murray. There's bound to be a contact address for them in the various volumes I've got," and Geoff immediately got up and made his way to his study.

A few minutes later an excited Geoff returned to the lounge clutching a well-read volume of Sir John's poems, "Here it is in the sleeve notes, the publisher's address."

Not renowned for leaving things to the last minute Geoff soon put pen to paper and two days later he posted a letter to Sir John Betjeman, complete with an enclosed stamped addressed envelope which would, he hoped, ensure a reply.

15th August 1975

Dear Sir John,

I hope you will forgive me for writing to you but I've been an admirer of your work for many years now. I well remember your radio talks on architecture and on West Coast towns

and cities, and over recent years I have
followed your programmes on television
with great interest. I have very fond
memories indeed of last year's 'A
Passion for Churches' and the previous
year's 'Metroland', both of which I
thoroughly enjoyed. I hope there will
be more such programmes to come in
the future.

My reason for writing to you is to
congratulate you on your LP entitled
'Betjeman's Banana Blush'. I only
recently stumbled upon this album and
have been completely captivated by it
and the subtle blending of your voice
with the music of Jim Parker. I find
all the tracks most stimulating and
thought provoking but one in
particular, 'Lenten Thoughts' has
particularly captivated me. So much
so that I would like to know more
about it.

The church in question obviously
moved you to the extent that you felt
compelled to write about it and one
person in particular who stood out from
the other worshipers. I would very much
like to visit this church and would be
grateful, therefore, if you could tell me
the name of the church and where it is
situated.

I look forward to hearing from you soon,

Yours sincerely,

Geoffrey Westbury

As the days turned into weeks Geoff began to despair that he wouldn't receive a reply from Sir John and that he would never solve the mystery of 'The Mistress'. His patience was rewarded, however, when a month later an envelope addressed in his own hand dropped through the letterbox early in the morning by the first post just as he was preparing to leave for work. He eagerly snatched it from the mat and almost ran into the kitchen to find the letter knife.

"It's here!" he exclaimed to Jackie who was sitting at the kitchen table thumbing through the newspaper, "He's replied, it's the letter from Sir John. It's typed but Sir John's signed it. I'll read it to you," and with trembling hands Geoff took the letter out of the envelope and nervously began to scan its contents.

20th September 1975

Dear Mr Westbury,

Thank you for your letter dated 15th August 1975.

I was delighted to learn that you have been an admirer of my work over the years and,

I must admit, your letter brought back many fond memories of my early days on radio.

The Banana Blush LP was a completely new venture for me. When the idea was first proposed I must admit I was rather sceptical but I'm very pleased with the end result and glad you enjoyed it. I think the music of Jim Parker captures the mood of the poems exquisitely and the two complement each other very well.

So far as 'Lenten Thoughts' is concerned I believe my inspiration for that particular poem came from a church in East Anglia, that I researched in preparation for 'A Passion for Churches', and one singular member of the congregation who stood out from the rest. It was as if she was floating on air without a care in the world and I wanted to try to capture that feeling of detachment, of otherworldliness, of sheer contentment.

The church featured in the poem is in the village of Booton Bassett which, if I recall correctly, is on the Suffolk coast. I hope you will take time to visit this charming little village and its church. I'm sure you'll be well rewarded.

Yours sincerely,

John Betjeman

Geoff read and reread the letter. He then realised the time, kissed Jackie goodbye and, carefully placing the letter in his briefcase, hurriedly left the house.

It was a very excited Geoff who returned home that evening clutching the latest 'A-Z' which he had purchased during his lunch break, and immediately announced, "I've found that village. Booton Bassett is on the Suffolk coast just a few miles south of Lowestoft. Why don't we drive up there at the weekend. We could have a look around, perhaps have a meal out; or even have a paddle in the sea."

"How far is it then? I don't fancy a long drive."

"Oh, it's only about 60 miles. We should be there in about an hour and a half. Looks like they're mainly 'A' roads but there are a few 'B' roads once we leave the A12."

"Well, we've nothing else planned, but I'll expect a decent meal. When do you want to go, Saturday or Sunday?"

"We'll go on Saturday. More chances of the shops being open and, if we decide to look around the church, we won't disturb the worshippers – unless there's a wedding or funeral!"

"Saturday it is, then," sighed Jackie and went into the kitchen to finish cooking the evening meal.

* * *

Saturday couldn't come soon enough for Geoff but, despite an early night, he didn't sleep very well and was up soon after seven o'clock. A bleary-eyed Jackie followed him down the stairs soon afterwards and was surprised to see that Geoff had almost finished getting the breakfast ready.

"You must be keen," she observed as she tucked into the bowl of cereal and, looking out of the window, added, "We've got a nice day. There's a bit of high cloud but lots of sunshine."

"It's a great day for exploring. We should get out more you know. If we enjoy today then we'll have to do it again."

"Perhaps, but not to the same place every time."

* * *

Soon after eight o'clock Geoff drove off the driveway and the car headed towards the A12 and the journey to Booton Bassett. As predicted by Geoff it took only 90 minutes to drive the 60 or so miles to this very pretty small Suffolk village.

Looking around Jackie observed, "So this is Booton Bassett. It looks very much like we've gone back in time a hundred years. Look at those quaint cottages painted in nice pastel colours, the village shop and Post Office, the old barns, and of course the village pub – 'The Half Moon' – we'll have lunch there. I bet they do some nice food. There's a blackboard outside with the menu written in chalk. There's bound to be something tempting on the menu."

Geoff found a place to park and the couple spent nearly an hour wandering around the village and savouring the atmosphere. "It's so tranquil here," said Jackie, "I'm almost glad I came!"

"But where's the church?" asked a slightly concerned Geoff who had suddenly remembered the purpose of their visit, "I can't see it anywhere. Did Sir John get it wrong?"

"No, of course he didn't," replied an exasperated Jackie, "If you look down the end of the village you can just see the tower rising above the trees. Come on, let's go and see what it's like," and she led the way along the winding narrow lane.

The church had been built in traditional East Anglian style, largely from flint and stone, and stood atop the cliffs adjacent to a building which helpfully had a sign on the door indicating it was the rectory. A short distance away stood what had at one time been a magnificent manor house but which was now no more than crumbling ruins covered in ivy and other invading vegetation.

"What a nice little church," remarked Geoff, "Not one of those vast churches built when this area was the centre of the wool trade, but a traditional Tudor church complete with its own rectory. And what a building that is. Those huge Tudor chimneys seem to dwarf the building. It must take a lot of money to maintain. I suppose the church was originally built in the grounds of the manor house so the Lord of the Manor didn't have to walk too far to worship. Wouldn't do to upset the Lord of the Manor," he joked. Then turning to Jackie said, "Let's go inside and have a look around. Hopefully the church will be open."

The church was indeed open and the two visitors went inside.

"Wow!" exclaimed Geoff, "What a find. This church seems to have survived both the zeal of Cromwell's Puritans for obliterating wall paintings and the Victorian's love of totally inappropriate and unwanted restoration. This must be very much how a church looked in late Tudor times; the rows of rich dark oak pews with a large enclosed pew at the front for the squire or Lord of the Manor to slumber in during the long boring sermons, the double-decker pulpit where the preacher would reserve the upper tier for those very important sermons, the fretworked chancel and rood screens and the stone font."

"Well summarised, my son!" and a mellow voice, seemingly emanating out of the ether, startled the visitors and caused them immediately to turn towards the door.

"I'm sorry if I surprised you but we don't get many visitors to our little church. If there is anything I can do or help you with please don't hesitate to ask. Oh, I'm sorry, let me introduce myself, I'm Simon Golightly, the rector of this parish."

"Pleased to meet you, rector," replied Geoff in a faltering voice, still recovering from the shock of the unexpected arrival, "This is my wife, Jackie, and I'm Geoff, Geoff Westbury."

"Welcome to Booton Bassett, and welcome to St Morwenna's, Booton Bassett's parish church. It's a pleasure to meet you both and I hope you enjoy looking around this ancient building. Don't forget you're in the house of God. I trust you will receive peace and inspiration from your visit here. Once you've finished in the church you can get a good lunch down at the pub. I often eat there myself – and enjoy the odd pint of locally brewed beer too. Everything in moderation of course. I'll let you carry on but, don't forget, you'll both be more than welcome at our Sunday worship. Services start at ten o'clock and I'd be delighted to welcome you into our family. By the way, if you explore the coast then please take care when up on the cliffs. As you can see they're largely unspoiled and over the years there have been a few terrible accidents, so please take care."

After the rector's departure Geoff and Jackie spent time looking at the inscriptions, wall paintings and effigies, and left the church feeling very calm and relaxed. They then went up on the cliffs behind the ruined manor house to experience the bracing North Sea air, then made their way back down into the village and finally made it to the pub.

"I could feel at home here," said Geoff as he finished an excellent meal, "But of course it's totally impractical. I'd never to able to commute to London; it's simply too far."

"Come on," responded Jackie, "Let's get you home before you decide to go to church here as well."

"That's not such a bad idea as it seems. I might even get to meet 'The Mistress!'"

Oddly enough, that remark of Jackie's stayed in Geoff's mind and he thought of nothing else on the rather uneventful journey home. His mind was filled with images of the church, not empty as he had seen it earlier in the day, but full of worshippers and bursting in song. It was as he pulled into his drive that he made a decision.

"Tomorrow," he announced to an incredulous Jackie, "I'm going back to Booton Bassett and that church. I'm going to take up that invitation from the rector and join him and his parishioners. Hopefully I will get to see 'The Mistress' and solve that enigma posed by Sir John. Perhaps then I'll be able to get that poem out of my mind once and for all!"

"Sometimes," frowned Jackie, "I regret buying you that LP. You seem to have become obsessed by it and with 'The Mistress' in particular. You'll be going on your own, you won't get me going to church."

Geoff, who was well aware of his wife's agnostic views, remained silent. He was, however, determined to revisit Booton Bassett and its little church the next day.

* * *

True to his word Geoff was up early the following day and left the house soon after eight o'clock. He kissed Jackie goodbye but she was barely awake and fell asleep once she heard the sound of the car leaving the drive.

Geoff arrived at Booton Bassett in good time for the service and ensconced himself in a pew near the front of the church. He stared around as the congregation arrived and filled nearly all of the pews. The service itself, conducted by the rector, Simon Golightly, was topical and lively and gave Geoff much food for thought. But all the time he was looking around at the members of the congregation, particularly the women; studying their clothes, peering into their faces, and looking for that illusive vision that was 'The Mistress'. It was not to be, however, and it was a very disappointed Geoff who shook hands with the rector as he left the church.

"I'm so glad you could join us," exclaimed the rector as he clasped Geoff's hand tightly, "Couldn't you persuade your wife to come with you?"

"Afraid not, rector, she does have an open mind but is something of an agnostic."

"Never mind, I'm sure she'll find what she's looking for," and staring Geoff straight in the eyes continued, "And so will you. You will find what you are searching for. We all do eventually, no matter how hard and distant it may seem at times."

Geoff would have liked to challenge the rector on this point but, as he was one in a line of people who were leaving the church and obviously looking forward to their Sunday lunches, he was forced to move on. He did, however, have much to reflect upon on the journey home. He had found the church but hadn't as yet found 'The Mistress' but he would keep trying. Perhaps next week. Yes, next week, he would come back to Booton Bassett the next Sunday and hope that the elusive 'Mistress' would put in an appearance.

Much to Jackie's sorrow and disappointment Geoff continued on his mission to Booton Bassett for the next few weeks and, despite taking up different pews each time and scanning the congregation from a number of vantage points, he was unable to identify anyone remotely resembling 'The Mistress'. This served only to increase his frustration and to make him more determined than ever to solve the mystery of just who this woman in the poem was. However, as the weeks rolled by and the winter months approached, the journey to Booton Bassett became more onerous and one he began to dread, particularly as the weather began to deteriorate.

"I think it's time you put an end to this. Admit it, you're never going to find out anything about this so called 'Mistress'," implored Jackie, "And besides, I worry about you driving all that way on your own when the weather's bad. It'll soon be Christmas so why not give it a break. Go up there again when the weather improves. After Easter it'll be much better. I might even go up with you. I did rather like that little village."

"Easter! That's it!" exclaimed Geoff rather loudly, "What a fool I've been. Don't you see, the clue is in the title of the poem, 'Lenten Thoughts'. Sir John was writing about something that he witnessed during Lent. That may explain why I haven't seen 'The Mistress'. Perhaps she only goes to that church during Lent. Now where did I put next year's calendar?" and Geoff left a rather bemused Jackie and hastily made his way to his study where, after rummaging amongst his papers, he eventually found his diary for 1976.

"Here we are," he said impatiently turning the pages, "The dates for Lent next year. It looks like the first Sunday in Lent is 7th March, the fifth Sunday in Lent is 4th April and Palm Sunday is on 11th April. That gives me six weeks in which to track down this elusive 'Mistress'.

"You're not seriously thinking of going all that way up there again next year are you?" an astounded Jackie remarked, "You're even more daft than I thought. Having read the works of Sir John, and many other poets, there's always the possibility that the whole episode didn't take place and was nothing more than a figment of his imagination. Let's face it, how do you know when a poet is writing from actual experience or simply as the result of a vivid imagination?"

"Sir John's letter. He clearly states that the events took place while he was researching 'A Passion for Churches' in Booton Bassett Parish Church; and I believe him."

"Have it your own way," resigned Jackie, and quietly returned to reading her book.

* * *

It was a long winter for Geoff and, try as hard as he might, 'Lenten Thoughts' and 'The Mistress' were never far from his thoughts. From mid-February onwards he began the countdown to that first Sunday in March which this year, 1976, also marked the first Sunday in Lent.

At last the appointed day dawned and Geoff set off in the car for Booton Bassett. Jackie had wisely declined his offer so he found himself once again alone with just his thoughts to keep him company. The drive along largely deserted roads seemed to go very quickly and, after what appeared to be no time at all, Geoff parked his vehicle in the car park at the end of the narrow lane that led up to the church.

"This is it," he thought as he took his place in a pew about half-way along the aisle and tried to relax as the church gradually began to fill up.

All through the service he kept a close eye on the congregation but didn't spot anyone who could possibly resemble Sir John's description of 'The Mistress'. Disappointment began to creep into his thoughts as the service came to an end and the congregation began slowly filing out of the church. Then suddenly there she was, 'The Mistress', elegantly gliding along the aisle towards the heavy oak door of the church.

"This must be her! But why didn't I spot her earlier? She must have been sitting in the front row! I must speak to her and find out if she knows she's the subject of one of the finest poems ever to flow from the pen of Sir John Betjeman."

But, try as he might, Geoff was unable to force his way through the throng intent on leaving the church. By the time he came to the door and out into the harsh late-winter sunshine the vision he saw gracefully floating down the aisle had vanished. He said but the briefest of words to the rector and searched the churchyard, the area leading up to the rectory, the grounds of the ruined manor house and the cliff path; but to no avail. There was no sign of 'The Mistress'. Rather despondently Geoff made his way back to the car but, deep down, he wasn't entirely unhappy. He had, finally, seen 'The Mistress'; proof at last, if he needed it, that she did indeed exist.

The Geoff that greeted his wife on his return was a very different person to the one who had left earlier in the day. His despondency had been replaced with a new sense of optimism and purpose.

"How did it go?" enquired Jackie, sensing a change in her husband.

"Better than ever I could have hoped. I believe I've seen 'The Mistress' as described with such passion by Sir John."

"Thank goodness for that. Perhaps our lives can revert to normal now and you can put all thoughts of that woman and that poem out of your mind." But Jackie couldn't resist asking, "What was she like?"

"Difficult to describe; she was a most striking woman, wearing a very elegant and expensive-looking two-tone crimson dress that had a sort of timeless quality to it. And, while most of the women in the church wore hats, she did not. It was difficult to tell inside the church but her eyes did appear to be a grey-green colour and they sparkled with a sort of mischievous quality as she glanced at those around her. As she passed the end of the pew she briefly looked towards me but there was no direct eye contact and it seemed as if she was unaware of her surroundings or who was present around her. There was almost a sort of magical quality about her and I can quite understand why her presence inspired Sir John to write his poem."

"No more trips up to Booton Bassett, then?" enquired Jackie.

"Quite the contrary. Now that I know she exists I must try and have a word with her. Ask her if she knows that she's the subject of one of Sir John's poems. Who knows, I might even get to know her name and where she lives."

Jackie was devastated, "I thought once you got to see this woman you'd be satisfied but no, you've still got to find out more. This has become an obsession and, if you're not careful, you'll turn into a stalker!"

"There's no fear of that," retorted Geoff, "I simply want to satisfy my curiosity. After all, there have been many instances in the past of people researching figures who have appeared in poems or literature and finding out about their background or circumstances, and that's all I intend to do."

True to his word, Geoff found himself back in Booton Bassett the following Sunday. This time he arrived early and positioned himself near the back of the church but, just before the service began, some late arrivals forced him to move in from the end of the pew. He eagerly studied all those coming into the church but he didn't catch a glimpse of 'The Mistress'. Saddened and fearing that he would be disappointed Geoff reluctantly participated in the service but, as the congregation began to file out of the church, there she was, 'The Mistress', walking towards him along the aisle in a very matter-of-fact way with just a hint of that enigmatic smile that made her so attractive.

Geoff endeavoured to force his way out of the pew but those next to him stood stubbornly still resisting his efforts to squeeze past. He watched as 'The Mistress' slowly glided past him and disappeared through the open door of the church. He managed to extricate himself from the pew but by the time he emerged into the open air he could see no trace of her.

"Very strange," he thought as he surveyed the crowd surging down the narrow lane, "Where on earth could she have gone so quickly? She's wearing that crimson dress again so should be very easy to spot."

Once again he had a quick look around the church grounds but to no avail; 'The Mistress' had eluded him for a second time.

Back home once more Geoff related his experience to Jackie who, by now, was having doubts about her husband's sanity. She tried to discourage him from his quest but, if Geoff had any enduring qualities, then persistence and sheer dogged determination summed him up perfectly. There was no doubt where he would be the coming Sunday morning and every following Sunday until he had managed to speak to 'The Mistress'.

The next three Sundays saw Geoff travel to Booton Bassett and on each occasion he had a similar experience. He would arrive in the church early, select a pew that allowed him to see clearly who was coming into the church and also provide him with a speedy exit; but to no avail. Every Sunday produced a familiar pattern; he never saw 'The Mistress' arrive but he did see her leave and, despite his best efforts, he failed to exit the church quickly enough to see where she went. He was also surprised to discover that she always wore the same dress, always had that enigmatic smile, always glanced about her as if looking for someone, and always managed to elude him.

The following Sunday, 11th April, was Palm Sunday and Geoff was determined that this time 'The Mistress' would not escape him; he had a plan that would allow him to speak to her at long last. He bid Jackie goodbye and drove to Booton Bassett with an air of positive anticipation.

* * *

"It's today or never," he affirmed, as he approached the small village along a 'B' road that he was so familiar with that he could, if necessary, drive along with his eyes closed, "Today's Palm Sunday and I'm certain that next Sunday, Easter Sunday, is not classed as being in Lent. I've got to make contact with that elusive 'Mistress' today. If not then I may have to wait another whole year and that would be unbearable."

It was a fine day but a strong onshore wind was blowing off the North Sea. Geoff sat in his parked car and deliberately left it to the last minute before entering the church. His plan was to go inside but, instead of sitting in one of the pews, remain standing at the back of the building. This would enable him to keep an eye on the congregation as it slowly filed out of the church and, as 'The Mistress' approached, he could then file out alongside her and, hopefully, strike up a conversation.

All started well and Geoff squeezed past the heavy oak door just as one of the church wardens was in the process of closing it. He took his place and made himself comfortable for what could be an hour to an hour-and-a-half's standing on a cold stone floor. However, a few minutes after the rector had commenced his welcoming address, he was aware of a hand on his arm and the church warden attempted to usher him to one of the pews. Geoff silently protested, and gestured to the church warden that he was happy to remain standing where he was, but to no avail. The church warden most firmly guided him to the end of a pew four rows from the door.

A reluctant Geoff had to remain seated throughout the service but, as it drew to a close, he became strangely agitated and couldn't wait for the congregation to begin to file out of the church. He eagerly scanned the throng of people moving slowly towards him and then, there she was, 'The Mistress', in her two-tone expensive-looking crimson dress, her face radiant with that smile of amused surprise so well described by Sir John, her sparkling grey-green eyes lighting up the church interior, coming ever closer to him. Geoff chose his moment well but, just before she reached him, a rather large woman in the row in front suddenly rose to her feet and forced 'The Mistress' to move over away from Geoff's pew. With 'The Mistress' briefly obscured from view he immediately got up, risked life and limb by pointedly pushing in front of the offending female, and joined the throng silently filing out of the church. 'The Mistress' was just two or three people in front of him; nothing could stop Geoff from approaching her once they were both outside.

"This is it," thought a jubilant Geoff as he braved the rather windy East-Anglian weather, "I hope she doesn't object to a short conversation with a stranger," but he hadn't reckoned on the Reverend Golightly.

"I'm so pleased you've become a regular member of our congregation. I was worried that we'd lost you when you didn't attend services during the winter but I'm pleased you've made a welcome return and joined us throughout Lent."

"Sorry Rector," stammered Geoff, "but I must have a word with that woman over there," and he pointed towards 'The Mistress' who was approaching the ruins of the manor house.

"Woman! What woman?" exclaimed the Rector, "There's nobody over there, just a pile of decaying stone that is testament to past glory and man's vanity. It's a sad truth that whatever we build will, in the long run, decay and return to where it came from, the earth, and that is the fate awaiting each and every one of us."

By this time, with his quarry almost out of view, Geoff was in no mood to have a philosophical conversation with the Rector. He quickly made his excuses and raced towards the ruins but, once there, he couldn't find any trace of 'The Mistress'; she had vanished completely. He slowly searched every inch of the ruins and the overgrown grounds but he had to admit defeat; once again 'The Mistress' had eluded him. Despondently he returned towards the church and met up again with the Rector who was walking towards the rectory.

"Did you find what you were looking for? Remember, the church is always open for quiet contemplation."

"I'm sorry, rector, but I was certain that a woman I was most anxious to speak to had gone over to the ruins but I couldn't find any trace of her. A most striking woman; she's been attending church throughout Lent and always wears the same expensive-looking two-tone crimson dress."

"A woman in a crimson dress you say. I think you must be mistaken. I face the congregation every Sunday morning and I know exactly who attends my church. I don't recall a woman of that description. Besides, why would she want to go over to the ruins of the old manor house? Nobody's lived there since the end of the First World War, 1918 I think my predecessor said."

Geoff was puzzled and enquired, "Who used to live there? It must have been a magnificent building in its heyday. It was obviously a wealthy family."

"Parts of the manor house date back to Tudor times. It was built for the deGroot family and the church and the rectory were built in its grounds at the same time. The deGroots were originally wealthy landowners but in Victorian times they branched into commerce and banking. Their fortune increased and they brought in the finest craftsmen and decorators from all over Europe to extend and improve the house. But, at the height of its glory disaster struck, and the house was abandoned and left to decay."

"What happened?" asked Geoff who, despite his initial ambivalence, was now becoming interested in the history of the ruined building.

"The last Lord of the Manor was Sir Alexander deGroot. He was a general in the army and received a posting to the front line early in 1918. Tragically, he was killed in a German gas attack towards the end of March that year. He was also the last of the deGroot line. Unfortunately, the story doesn't end there. Alexander and his wife Georgiana were apparently very close and utterly devoted to each other. When the telegraph boy delivered the telegram informing her of her husband's death Georgiana was devastated and couldn't cope with the loss. Just a few days later in deep despair and grief, oddly enough I believe it was on Palm Sunday, she attended church as usual. Immediately afterwards, however, she made her way up to the top of the cliffs. She stood silently for several minutes looking over the edge towards the rocks and the sea below and then, as the rector approached to try and comfort her, she jumped and plunged into the water. Her body was swept out to sea in the strong currents and never recovered."

"A sad story indeed," reflected Geoff, and after a brief pause added, "But I suppose I should be going. Don't want to take up more of your time."

"Not at all. Tell you what. Why don't you come back to the rectory with me for a cup of tea. I've got a collection of old photographs showing just how grand and splendid the manor house used to be. There are even some old paintings of the building and some portraits of former Lords of the Manor which I'm sure will interest you."

"All right," replied Geoff, exhibiting a renewed interest, "That sounds very intriguing and the tea would be most welcome," and the two men slowly walked towards the rather spooky-looking rectory braving the strong easterly winds.

Geoff spent a very pleasant hour with the Reverend Golightly. The Manor House, in its prime, was indeed a most beautiful building set in extensive grounds bordered by neatly manicured lawns and well stocked gardens. It was hard to reconcile it with the present-day ruins surrounded by overgrown weeds and creepers.

As the rector escorted Geoff towards the front door he suddenly stopped, "I almost forgot," he said most apologetically, "I've got a couple of other portraits in the study which might interest you," and he led Geoff into a small room which was almost covered from floor to ceiling in bookshelves, "There! What do you think of those portraits? On the left is Alexander deGroot, the last Lord of the Manor, and on his right is his wife, Georgiana."

Geoff froze, he couldn't take his eyes off the portrait of Georgiana and stood rooted to the spot, speechless, in sheer disbelief. He was looking at none other than 'The Mistress'! Her full-length portrait gazed down at him through those bright grey-green eyes and her partially open mouth reflected that hint of surprise that made her so attractive and mysterious. And most remarkable of all, she was wearing that expensive-looking, but timeless, two-tone crimson dress. Here at last was what he had been searching for. But could he really believe that this woman, who had been dead for nearly sixty years, had visited this very church every Sunday morning during Lent? And why did the rector say he hadn't seen her there? Surely he must have noticed her?

Geoff had many questions. He desperately wanted to tell the Reverend Golightly of his search, his pilgrimage if the truth was acknowledged, but he decided to remain silent.

"Beautiful, isn't she?" Sighed the rector, "They say she was wearing that dress on the day she died. What can I say? What comfort could my predecessor have possibly given her? I suppose we'll never know what went through her mind on that fateful day. I like to think that she and Alexander, who were so close in life, are now together in death. Still, that's enough of my musings. You must want to get along and back to your wife; you have a long journey ahead of you."

Geoff walked slowly back to his car reflecting on the morning's events. His curiosity had at last been satisfied, he had discovered the identity of 'The Mistress', but in a most unexpected and unimaginable way. He knew he would never return to Booton Bassett. He knew he would never see 'The Mistress' again but he also knew that he had been privileged to glimpse something special. Something he could not mention to anybody else, including Jackie.

* * *

On that very morning, over a hundred miles away in his London office, Sir John Betjeman was undertaking some spring cleaning and was in the process of throwing out some unwanted draft manuscripts and papers. He was casually screwing up papers and dropping them in a waste paper basket when his attention was drawn to a letter he had received from a certain Geoffrey Westbury over six months previously. For a few minutes he studied both the letter and his reply then very slowly and deliberately folded them into four and carefully placed them in the basket. He sat silently for a short while and then with a mischievous smile mused, "I wonder if he ever made the effort to visit that village of Booton Bassett and its charming little church. I hadn't the heart to tell him that it was my researcher who went there and not me. And as for 'The Mistress'; well, she doesn't exist. She was just a figment of my imagination!"

The End

Home Sweet Home

HOME SWEET HOME

(A tragedy in two acts)

Act one and a youngish couple, Robin and Donna, run panting and very much out of breath up to the front door of a house. It's clear they've been running very hard, as if they are being pursued by someone.

They stand gasping for breath as Robin fumbles in his pocket for the key.

"Hurry up for God's sake!" shouts Donna with obvious signs of panic, "Open that blasted door, quickly, or we'll be caught! Come on! Now!"

"I'm trying to find the damn key," Robin replies, producing the small front door key at last, and he thrusts it into the keyhole and turns it vigorously.

"Get in!" he shouts as the door opens and he roughly pushes Donna into the hall. He quickly follows and, once inside, immediately slams the door shut.

Side-by-side they both lean with their backs firmly against the door catching their breath and trying to calm down.

"Made it," exclaims Donna. "I really thought our luck had run out this time. Let's have a drink." And they make their way, still trembling, into the kitchen.

Donna puts the kettle on and Robin fetches a couple of mugs from a cupboard. As they sit down at the kitchen table they hear a noise outside.

"What was that?" exclaims a startled and worried Donna, "She's found us!"

"No, it must have been the wind," replies Robin reassuringly and, looking up, says, "I can't see anything out the window. All the same, we'd better check the doors and windows." And they both go hand-in-hand, obviously very afraid of someone or something, into all the downstairs rooms and check that all the windows and outside doors are securely fastened.

Satisfied that everything is safe and secure they breathe a sigh of relief and go into the lounge and sit next to each other on the sofa.

"Safe at last," sighs a relieved Donna, "I never thought we'd make it back."

Suddenly, there's a loud knock on the front door.

"Don't open it! Don't even go and see who's there!" exclaims a very worried-looking Donna and she cuddles up to Robin who hugs her reassuringly.

Soon there's another loud knock on the front door and the couple embrace each other tighter, fear showing visibly on their faces.

After a pause there's a knock on the back door and, when that isn't answered, there's a rattling on the windows. At this point Robin and Donna dive behind the sofa and, just as they do so, a large shadow is cast over the lounge window and the glass rattles in its frame.

There's another short pause then a fierce banging is heard on the front door. This is followed by repeated large thuds, a creaking sound as pressure is applied to the door, and finally the sound of wood splintering as the door eventually gives way and crashes onto the floor of the hallway. Robin and Donna freeze. They remain lying on the floor absolutely still with a look of sheer terror on their faces.

Act two and the scene immediately shifts to a little girl, aged about 8 or 9 years, playing with her dolls' house. She looks very angry indeed. She reaches inside the dolls' house and forcibly brings out two dolls, dressed in exactly the same clothes as Robin and Donna, and holds them up in front of her face.

"You've been naughty again! What have I told you?" She stamps her feet and shrieks at the top of her voice, shaking the dolls repeatedly. "No more games of hide and seek for you! I've tried to find you everywhere. You've been very naughty and now you've got to be punished." And, without uttering a further word, she violently pulls the heads off the two dolls, throws them onto the floor and stomps off in a tantrum.

The End

Lightning Source UK Ltd.
Milton Keynes UK
UKHW010640171121
394121UK00001B/98